Jacob Abbott

Stories of Rainbow and Lucky

Jacob Abbott

Stories of Rainbow and Lucky

ISBN/EAN: 9783743393660

Manufactured in Europe, USA, Canada, Australia, Japa

Cover: Foto ©Andreas Hilbeck / pixelio.de

Manufactured and distributed by brebook publishing software (www.brebook.com)

Jacob Abbott

Stories of Rainbow and Lucky

STORIES

OF

RAINBOW AND LUCKY.

BY

JACOB ABBOTT.

NEW YORK:

HARPER & BROTHERS, PUBLISHERS,

FRANKLIN SQUARE.

1860.

STORIES

OF

RAINBOW AND LUCKY.

ORDER OF THE VOLUMES.

STORIES

OF

RAINBOW AND LUCKY.

THE THREE PINES.

CONTENTS.

ENGRAVINGS.

THE THREE PINES.

Arrival at Southerton.	Long hill.

IT was nearly ten o'clock at night when Handie and Rainbow arrived in the wagon at the town of Southerton, where the farm of The Three Pines was situated. When they were about two miles from the town they came to the foot of a hill, which seemed to continue to ascend for a long distance before them. Tolie, the boy who was driving them, and who was seated on a box which had been placed in the front of the wagon, let the reins fall slack upon the horse's back as soon as they began the ascent, and said,

"Here we are at the long hill. Now we shall soon be at Southerton."

"Is it a very long hill?" asked Handie.

"It is nearly half a mile from here to the top of it," said Tolie. "It goes winding through the woods all the way."

"I will get out and walk up," said Handie.

"Oh no," said Tolie; "the horse is not tired." "I am going to walk up for my own sake, and not for his," replied Handie; and, so saying, without waiting for Tolie to stop the wagon, he leaped out into the road.

"And I'll get out too," said Rainbow.

"No," replied Handie. "Don't get out because I do. I want a little exercise, that's all. If you and Tolie are comfortable where you are, sit still."

Rainbow *was* perfectly comfortable. He was always comfortable when he was riding. So Handie walked on, leaving Tolie and Rainbow to follow in the wagon.

"This is a lonely kind of place," said Rainbow.

"It is not very lonely now," said Tolie, "because the moon shines so bright among the trees. But I've driven through here in dark nights when it was lonely enough, and all I could do to find my way was to follow the narrow strip of sky in the opening of the trees overhead. Whichever way that turned I knew the road turned. All below in the road each side of it was as dark and black as a coal-hole in a dark cellar."

"Could you contrive to follow the road in that way?" asked Rainbow.

"Pretty well," said Tolie. "And, besides, I watched the level of the wagon, and if the wheels began to go down too much on one side, I'd haul off more to the other, so as to keep out of the gutters."

"You ought to have a lantern for such a dark night as that," said Rainbow.

"I don't like a lantern," said Tolie, "it is so much trouble to hold it."

"Is not there any place where you could fasten it up?" asked Rainbow.

"No," said Tolie. "And, besides, it is only while we are going through the woods that there is any trouble. We can always find our way well enough in the open country."

"But suppose you meet any body going through the woods?" asked Rainbow.

"Why, we don't very often meet any body such dark nights. Nobody travels then if they can possibly help it."

"But *sometimes* you meet people, I suppose," said Rainbow.

"Yes," said Tolie, "sometimes. Once I met a fellow from Southerton coming down this hill when I could not see any thing at all. I heard his wagon wheels and his horses' feet plashing through the mud. I sung out to him to keep to the right. 'Keep to the right,' says

I, 'as the law directs.'   He sung out, 'Ay, ay ;' and when he got opposite to me, I knew he was going by by the sound which the wheels made, dripping along through the mud, but I could not see any thing at all.   'Hallo!' says I. 'Hallo!' says he.   'Take a good look at me,' says he, 'so as to be sure that you'll know me when you see me again.'   So he cracked his whip and went on ; but, just as he passed me, he called back again, and said, 'Look out and not lose your bosom-pin,' says he: 'it is just ready to drop out.'"

Here Tolie laughed aloud at the recollection.

"What did he mean about the bosom-pin?" asked Rainbow.   Rainbow was not particularly quick in taking a joke.

"Oh, it was only his fun," said Tolie, "pretending to see such small things when it was so dark.   I hadn't any bosom-pin."

Thus the two boys rode on, talking together in a very sociable manner, until they had got about half way up the hill, when Tolie asked Rainbow who Handie was.

"Who is this boy," said he, "that you are traveling with?"

"It is not a boy," said Rainbow ; "it is a man.   His name is Mr. Level."

"Yes," replied Tolie, "I heard you call him Mr. Level, but he is not a man any more than I am. He is not more than eighteen or nineteen years old, is he?"

"He is nineteen," said Rainbow; "but then he has bought his time of his father, and so he is free. Still, people sometimes call him Handie, for that was his name when he was a boy."

"Where did he get his money to buy his time?" asked Tolie.

"I've heard say he borrowed it," replied Rainbow.

"Hoh!" said Tolie, "he could not borrow enough. A fellow's time, when he's only nineteen, and there's two years more to run, is worth more than a hundred dollars, if he's good for any thing at all to work, and nobody would lend him so much money."

"But Handie Level is different," said Rainbow; "he can borrow as much money as he wants. Any body will lend it to him. Besides, he owns this farm."

"What farm?" asked Tolie.

"This farm of The Three Pines, where he is going now to work. His uncle, that died a little while ago, left it to him by a will."

"And is he going to live there?" asked Tolie.

"No," said Rainbow, "he is only going now to put it in repair. The place has run down a good deal, and, as he is a carpenter by trade, they have sent him to put it in order. And I am going to help him," added Rainbow, proudly.

"*Who* has sent him to put it in order?" asked Tolie.

"Squire James," replied Rainbow. "He is the trustee or something. You see, the place does not really come to Handie for some time yet, because he is too young to have a farm. But he is just as much interested in it as if he was going to live there now. He'll put it all in first-rate order, you may depend. He's an excellent carpenter."

"And are you a carpenter too?" asked Tolie.

"No," replied Rainbow, "I am only going to help about the rough work. But I mean to learn all about the trade that I can."

"Where are your tools?" asked Tolie.

"They are in the chest back here where the stage upset," replied Rainbow. "There is a chest of tools, and a trunk with all our clothes in it. The driver is going to bring them on to-night."

About this time the wagon reached the top of the hill, where Handie was found sitting by the road-side on a stone, waiting for it. When

he got in, he began to speak of the arrangements to be made for the night.

"Trigget will be coming by very early in the
morning," said he, "and he is going to leave our
baggage at the door, and I ought to be there to
receive it. If I were sure there was any hay or
straw in the barn, you and I would stop at The
Three Pines, and sleep there to-night ourselves."

"You may be pretty sure there is *not* any
hay or straw there," said Tolie.

"Why so?" asked Handie.

"The folks that lived there would not be
likely to leave much when they went away,"
said Tolie; "and if only a little were left, it
would be gone long ago, with Ma'am Blooman
living next door."

"Who is Ma'am Blooman?" asked Handie.

"She is the crossest and ugliest old vixen in
town," said Tolie. "She lives in the next
house. You may depend upon it, you will not
find any hay or straw in your barn."

"We can't sleep very well on the bare
boards," said Handie, musing.

"*I* can get plenty of straw for you," said
Tolie.

"Where?" asked Handie.

"Oh, at any of the farmers' along the road
here," said Tolie.

B

18   THE THREE PINES.

Mr. Workworth's.   Buying straw.   The four bundles.

"Very well," said Handie; "that will just be what we want."

"Here's Mr. Workworth's, the next house," said Tolie. "He's got some, I don't doubt."

Just as the wagon came opposite to Mr. Workworth's house the door opened, and a man came out with a lantern in his hand, and moved toward the barn.

"There's Joe Workworth now, going to the barn," said Tolie, "to give the cattle the last foddering." Then, calling out aloud, he said,

"Joe!"

"Hallo!" answered Joe.

"We want some straw," said Tolie.

"Very well," said Joe, "you can have it."

"Well, bring it along, then," said Tolie.

"How much do you want?" asked Joe.

"Four bundles," said Handie, in a low tone, to Tolie.

"Four bundles," repeated Tolie, calling out the number aloud to Joe.

So Joe went on and entered the barn. In a short time he appeared again, with the straw loaded on his shoulders and head, so that he looked like a moving hay-cock. He came to the wagon, and put the bundles in behind.

"Tolie," said he, "is that you?"

They drive on.

"So they say," said Tolie. "How 'much is to pay?"

Joe said that the straw was six cents a bundle. Handie took the money out of his pocket and paid what was due, and then, bidding Joe good-by, Tolie drove on.

CHAPTER II.
POOR ACCOMMODATIONS.

AT length the sight of a spire and a cupola rising above a group of roofs of houses and of trees indicated to the travelers their approach toward the village. The village began thus to appear in view just as the wagon came out of a wood. In the edge of the wood, or, rather, on the margin of the open land which bordered upon it, on the right-hand side of the road, was a small wooden house, with a barn and shed attached to it, and a little garden behind. There was a light in one of the windows of the house, and Handie could see the shadow of somebody coming to the window to look out as the wagon drove by.

"That is Ma'am Blooman's house," said Tolie, "and that is she herself looking out at the window. The next house is yours."

Of course Handie looked forward very earnestly at the next house. He could see it pretty distinctly by the light of the moon. There was a pretty broad field between Mrs. Blooman's house and his, with a few trees growing here and there against the fence. These trees at first concealed the house in some degree, but presently it came into full view. It was a one-story house, painted red. It stood back a little way from the road, and the front of it looked toward a large open yard on the farther side of it. Handie saw that the situation of it was pleasant.

There was a small yard, inclosed in an ornamental fence, on the side of the house toward the road, though there was no door leading into the house on that side. Indeed, strictly speaking, it was an end of the house that was turned toward the road. Tolie, of course, drove on till he had passed beyond the house, and then turned up into the large open yard, and stopped before the front door.

"I don't know how you are going to get in," said he.

"Oh, we'll contrive some way to get in," said Handie. "All you have to do is to set us down and to wait till Rainbow takes out the straw, and then you may go. We will take care of ourselves."

As Handie stepped down from the wagon he saw that the open yard extended behind the house, and that it was inclosed in that direction by several large sheds and barns. The ground all over the yard was covered with chips and litter. Handie took a rapid survey of the place, and then turned to see about unloading the straw. Rainbow took the bundles out one after another, and laid them down near the porch, in a place which Handie designated.

"I think you had better go to the tavern with me, after all," said Tolie. "The house is all fastened up."

"We'll *try* to get in, at any rate," said Handie. "If we should not succeed, we can come to the tavern ourselves by-and-by."

Accordingly Tolie, after the straw had been all unloaded, took his place on the regular seat, which Handie and Rainbow had hitherto occupied, turned the horse round by taking a great sweep over the chips in the back yard, and went away.

"Now, Rainbow," said Handie, "we will make a survey."

So he began to walk about the house, trying the different doors and looking up at the windows. All the doors were fastened, as were also all the lower windows.

"We must contrive some way," said Handie, "to get up to one of the chamber windows. I don't believe that they are fastened. Let us go and look into the sheds, and see what we can find there.

"Yes," said Rainbow, "we may perhaps find a ladder, and that will be exactly the thing."

They looked through the sheds, and also went into one of the barns, but it was too dark to see much. There was no ladder to be found. Rainbow opened a barn door so as to let a little moonlight in, but there was nothing of any consequence inside. He saw on a beam a small earthen jar, and by the side of it a tin mug, and also an old, worn-out curry-comb.

"That jar would have been a good thing for me to have packed my pond-lily roots in," said Rainbow.

"Take it down, if you can," said Handie, "and see what there is in it."

Rainbow took down the jar, and, after looking into it, said that it was full of wheel-grease.

"Very good," said Handie. "That is just what we shall want by-and-by."

Rainbow could not well imagine what Handie could want of wheel-grease at such a time, but he forbore to ask any questions.

Handie then returned into the shed, and, stopping at a door which led from the shed to a sort of calf-pen next the barn, he asked Rainbow to help him lift the door off its hinges.

The hinges were of such a form that this could easily be done.

They carried the door out into the yard, and by means of it Handie contrived to get up to a chamber window over the kitchen. The way in which he managed it was this. Handie and Rainbow placed the door in an upright position against the house, opposite the lower window. They placed the door at right angles to the house—that is, with the inner edge of it against the wall, and the other edge standing out, like a door wide open. Handie put something under the outer corner of the door to give it a firm foundation to rest upon, and then gave it in charge to Rainbow to hold it steadily in its place while he climbed up upon it.

Handie succeeded, much to Rainbow's surprise, in climbing up without any difficulty. He took hold of the door to assist himself in his ascent, while Rainbow held it still in its place, and then, stepping first on the sill of the lower window, he climbed up, until at last he got upon the upper edge of the door, where he steadied himself by taking hold of the sill of the upper window. While standing in this position he contrived to push the sash of the upper window up—for, as he had expected, it was not fastened—and then he climbed in.

GETTING INTO A HOUSE.

As soon as he was in he turned round and said that he had done with the door, and told Rainbow that he might take it away to its place, and lean it against the partition there, ready to be put upon its hinges again.

When Rainbow came back from carrying away the door, he found Handie opening the back door of the house from the inside, and coming out.

"Now, Rainbow," said Handie, "the first thing is to build a fire in the kitchen fireplace. We want a fire, not for the warmth of it, but to drive the spooks out of the house."

What Handie meant by driving the spooks out of the house was to dispel the lonesomeness, and make it look cheerful and pleasant. Even Rainbow knew that there was really no such things as spooks, either in a lonely house or any where else.

"Look around the yard," said Handie, "and pick me up some chips and kindling, and I'll strike a light and make a fire."

Rainbow immediately set himself at work, and in a short time went into the house, carrying in an armful of chips, sticks, and pieces of wood of all kinds. With these Handie soon made a great blazing fire, which threw a very bright light all over the room, and gave to the

whole interior an extremely cheerful and ani-
mated aspect.

Handie then sent Rainbow out to bring in
the bundles of straw, and then he spread the
straw down so as to make two beds along the
back side of the room, as far as possible from
the fire.

" Now, Rainbow," said he, " all that we want
is a lamp. You see, our fire will go down in
the night while we are asleep. Besides, I am
curious to look about in the other rooms a little. Go out into the barn and bring me that
jar of wheel-grease and the old tin mug which
stands by the side of it on the beam ; and
in going and coming, look all about the yard,
and see if you can find any little bit' of cotton
rag."

In due time Rainbow returned from the barn,
bringing the jar with him in one hand, and the
mug and some white rags in the other. He
found Handie standing before the fire, at work
with his knife upon a small piece of wood.
The wood was flat and thin, and about as large
round as a silver dollar. Handie had shaped
it in that manner by the light of the fire, and
was now boring a hole through the centre of it
with the point of his knife.   .

" I am making a float," said he to Rainbow

as Rainbow came in, "to hold the wick of our lamp."

When he had finished boring the hole, he took the rag which Rainbow had brought in, and having cut off a small piece of it, he rolled it up into a little roll about as large as the wick of a lamp. He put one end of this roll through the hole in the float, and then cut off the two ends of it, each about half an inch from the wood.

"Rather a short lamp-wick," said Rainbow.

"Yes," replied Handie; "but we only want it to last through this one night. We will have a better lamp to-morrow."

While Handie was adjusting the wick, Rainbow took out a quantity of the grease from the jar by means of a small stick shaped like a paddle which he found in the jar, and which was used for applying the grease to the axles of wheels, and filled the mug with it. Handie then put the little float on the top of it, having first made a small hole to receive the lower end of the wick. He then melted a little of the grease in the fire, and wet the upper end of the wick with it, and finally, using a thin splinter of wood for a match, he lighted his lamp. Rainbow, much to his surprise, found that it burned very well, and gave an excellent light.

Inspection.

"Now, Rainbow," said Handie, as soon as the lamp began to burn steadily and clear, "we will make a little exploring tour about our house, and see what we can find."

CHAPTER III.

EXPLORING.

RAINBOW was very glad to hear Handie propose to make an exploration of the house before going to bed. He was a little inclined to be afraid to go to sleep in such a lonesome place, and he thought that he should feel much more at his ease if, before going to bed, they should first visit all the rooms, in order to be sure that there was nothing in them that ought not to be there. He did not really think that there were any spooks to be feared, but he imagined that perhaps some crazy man, or drunken man, might have strayed into the house, or even that thieves or robbers might have taken possession of it in its deserted condition. Indeed, he was almost afraid to go into the rooms to see, even with Handie to go before him and carry the lamp. He would have been quite afraid to have gone alone.

Handie, however, who had no such thoughts in his head, but was influenced only by curiosity to see what sort of rooms he should find, and what the disposition of them was, took the

mug lamp in his hand, and led the way while
Rainbow followed.   From the kitchen they
went through a small entry which led to a front
room, that appeared to be the sitting-room, or
best room of the house.   It had three windows
in it, two on one side and one on the other.
The two windows looked out toward the road.
The other window was toward the side yard,
where the wagon had come in.

The room was in great disorder.   The fireplace was filled with ashes and half-burned
brands, and the floor was covered with litter.
The boards, too, were loose here and there, the
latches were broken, and one of the doors was
half off its hinges.

" There will be some work for us to do here,"
said Handie.

From this room Handie passed through a
door which it was very difficult to open on account of its rubbing so hard upon the floor, to
another room behind it, which Handie said he
thought must have been intended for a bedroom.   There were large closets in it for clothes,
but the shelves were almost all gone from them.
There were two broken panes of glass in one
of the windows, and a large place in one corner
of the room where the plastering had fallen
down from the ceiling overhead.

"We shall find that there is a leak in the roof over that corner, I suppose," said Handie.

"Is that what makes the plastering fall?" asked Rainbow.

"Yes," replied Handie, "that is generally the cause. A leak in a roof usually makes a great deal of mischief."

In the back part of the bedroom there was a door leading again into the kitchen, through a small entry that was between.

"Ah!" exclaimed Handie, when he came to this door, "this makes it very convenient. My wife. when I bring her home by-and-by to live with me in this house, will like this very much. She can go into her parlor or into her kitchen, whichever she pleases, directly from her bedroom."

"That will be very handy," said Rainbow.

The door that led into the kitchen from the bedroom was entirely off its hinges, and stood leaning up against the opening. Handie moved it aside in order that he and Rainbow might go through, and then replaced it again. They then passed out from the kitchen through a door which led into a sort of wash-room or back kitchen. Just as they entered this room, Rainbow was startled to see something white dashing through a broken panel in a door

C

which seemed to lead out toward the sheds and barns.

" What's that ?" said he, quite frightened.

" It was a cat," replied Handie. " I verily believe it was a cat. Let us get something, and see if we can't coax her back."

So he went into the kitchen again, opened the bundle which Rainbow had brought along the road, and took out a parcel from his portion of it. The parcel was wrapped up in paper. On opening the parcel, it was found to contain three crackers packed in a bright and new tin mug, a small pie, and a pretty large piece of cheese.

" There is nothing here that she will like," said Handie, " unless it be the cheese. She may like a piece of that, if she is very hungry."

Handie cut off a piece of the cheese with his knife, and gave it to Rainbow.

" Here, Rainbow," said he, " take this cheese and the lamp, and see if you can coax her back, while I build up the fire."

So Rainbow went out to the back room again, and, looking through the broken panel where pussy had made her escape, he saw two bright eyes peering in upon him from the darkness there.

He immediately began to call pussy, and to hold out his cheese; but on the instant that his voice was heard the eyes disappeared.

He waited patiently a few minutes, calling all the time in a kind and gentle tone, and presently the eyes appeared again. Rainbow remained where he was, and continued to call. The cat came forward a little, and put her fore paws upon the edge of the board where the panel had been broken out. She looked into the room, but did not seem to dare to come in.

Rainbow tossed a small piece of the cheese toward her, and, at the same time, fell back a little himself toward the kitchen door. The cat watched the cheese for a moment, looking alternately at that and at Rainbow, and when she saw that Rainbow had retreated to a safe distance, she came in cautiously, crept up to the cheese, seized it, and then, turning suddenly, ran back and disappeared.

Rainbow waited patiently where he was, without moving or speaking a word, and pretty soon pussy reappeared. Rainbow began to call her again, at the same time holding out another piece of cheese toward her. Presently she stepped cautiously over into the room, and began walking back and forth, rubbing her head and back against the door, being evidently desirous of making farther acquaintance with Rainbow, but yet afraid to do so. Rainbow, however, did not advance toward her, but remained motionless where he was, and at length gradually succeeded in inducing her to come to him. He allowed her to eat two or three pieces of cheese before he attempted to touch her, and then he put his hand gently upon her head, and stroked the fur down upon her back. After this he took her up in his arms, and went back with her into the kitchen.

In the mean time Handie had brought in two blocks of wood which he found out in the yard, and, by placing the blocks by the side of the fire at a little distance apart, and laying the board across from one to the other, he made a very good seat. The fire was quite pleasant, for, as the night advanced, the air became cool. Handie and Rainbow sat down upon the seat, and ate the rest of the crackers and cheese, and also the pie. Rainbow kept the cat in his lap all the time, and gave her a liberal portion of his share.

For drink they had some water, which Handie contrived to get from the well by means of his bright mug; for the windlass was broken, and they could not draw the water in the ordinary way. Handie made a long string from the strands of a piece of rope which Rainbow found in the barn, and with this he let the mug down twice, pulling it up each time full of water. Rainbow let the mug down the third time to draw up some for his cat, but this proved to be unnecessary, for the cat did not appear to be thirsty.

"I wish we knew the name of our cat," said Rainbow. "Do you suppose that she belonged to the family who lived here last?"

"She belonged to the *house*, I suppose, rather than to the family," replied Handie. "Cats belong to places rather than to persons. So, you see, when the family went away she staid. If she had been a dog she would have gone away with them."

"At any rate," said Rainbow, "I wish I knew what her name was."

"You must give her a new one," said Handie.

"Very well," said Rainbow; "what shall it be?"

"Can't you think of something connected with pines, so as to denote that she belongs to The Three Pines farm?" asked Handie.

"Pine-apple," said Rainbow. "We might call her Pine-apple."

"Very good," replied Handie. "You could not have any better name."

It is true that the pine-apple, so called, is not
the produce of the pine by any means, but of a
plant entirely different from it in all respects.
But this seemed of no consequence to Handie,
so long as there was an analogy in the name.
He did not seem to think that precise etymo-
logical accuracy was of any essential import-
ance in naming a cat.

After this Handie and Rainbow went to bed.
They did not undress themselves, for they had
no sheets to spread upon the straw, nor any
blankets to put over them. So they lay down
in their clothes, just as they were. Before lying down, however, they replenished the fire by
packing in some wood as closely as possible
on the hearth, and covering it up in a great
measure with ashes, so as to make it burn slowly. They put their lamp, too, on the mantel-
piece, and left it burning there. The last thing
that Rainbow saw before he went to sleep was
Pine-apple lying comfortably in the chimney-
corner, and looking into the fire with a countenance expressive of great content and satisfaction.

HANDIE'S ARRANGEMENTS. 39

The stage comes with the baggage.   Pleasant morning.   Dew.

CHAPTER IV.

HANDIE'S ARRANGEMENTS.

RAINBOW knew nothing after this for several hours. He was awakened at length by the sound of wheels driving up and stopping before the house. He opened his eyes and looked about him, and found that Handie was gone. He immediately got up, and, as he was already dressed, he had nothing to do but to put on his cap. He then went out to the front door, and there he found, as he had expected, that the stage had come, and that the driver was taking off Handie's trunk and tool-chest. He hastened to the place to help. When the baggage had been set down, he took first the trunk, and then the tool-chest, and brought them to the house, leaving Handie talking to the driver. In a few minutes the stage drove on.

It was after sunrise, and the morning was very pleasant.

"I should like to take a walk with you about my farm now before breakfast," said Handie, "and see how it looks; but the dew is so heavy

40   THE THREE PINES.

Plans for the day.   Shop.   The tool-chest.   Going to breakfast.

on the grass that we should find it very wet.
So we will wait until this evening, and go when
our day's work is done. Besides, there are a
great many things to be done to-day in order
to get ready for me to go to work regularly to-
morrow, and 'Duty first, pleasure afterward,' is
the rule."

So Handie and Rainbow went to work immediately, clearing up the ground and putting
things in order. Handie himself, after having
set Rainbow at work about the yard, went to
select a place to be used as his shop. At first
he thought of taking one of the rooms in the
house for this purpose; but he reflected that
that would not be convenient, on account of
the difficulty of getting boards, and long stuff
generally, in and out. Then he thought of the
barn; but he concluded that he might perhaps
have occasion to use the barn to drive some
team in, or for the storage of lumber. Finally he decided upon the back room behind the
kitchen, and Rainbow assisted him to carry his
tool-chest there.

At seven o'clock, Handie, taking Rainbow
with him, went into the village to the tavern
in order to get some breakfast. After breakfast Handie sent Rainbow back to the house
again, while he himself went to see a certain

gentleman to whom he had a letter from Mr. James. Mr. James had made an arrangement with this gentleman to render Handie any assistance he might require, and to pay him money from time to time, both for purchases of lumber and hardware for his repairs, and also for his and Rainbow's wages every Saturday night.

About the middle of the forenoon, while Rainbow was at the house engaged in doing the work which Handie had assigned him, a team drove into the yard, loaded with planks, boards, joists, shingles, and other lumber. Rainbow helped the teamster to discharge his load, and he piled the various kinds of stuff, each sort by itself, upon the barn floor, in such a situation as to make it all easily accessible. When at length Handie returned, he was very much pleased with the disposition which Rainbow had made of it all.

Handie immediately went to work to make his bench. He selected from the different sorts of lumber that were in the barn the pieces of stuff that were necessary for his purpose, and Rainbow helped him take them from the piles.

When this was done, Handie said,

"And now, Rainbow, I can saw out the stuff for my bench myself, though I shall need you

to help me put the bench together when I get
it all ready. In the mean time, I want you to
sweep the whole house out from top to bottom.
I shall make a great litter of chips and shavings in all the rooms myself, I know, but I want
the old litter all cleared out first, so as to begin
fresh and new. Besides, carpenter's litter is
clean litter, and what is there now is dirt."

"Yes," said Rainbow, "it is best to clean the
rooms all out."

"But what shall we do for a broom?" said
Handie. "I have not got any broom."

"Might we not borrow one of some of the
neighbors?" suggested Rainbow.

"No," said Handie, shaking his head, "I
don't wish to begin my dealings with the neighbors by borrowing of them—nor if I can help
it."

"I can make a hemlock broom," said Rainbow, "if that would do."

"That will do very well," said Handie. "Do
you think you could go into the woods somewhere and get some hemlock?"

"Yes," said Rainbow; "there are plenty of
firs and hemlocks in the woods beyond Mrs.
Blooman's house."

"Very well," replied Handie; "go and get
some hemlock stuff, enough for one or two

brooms, and while you are gone I'll make a handle."

So Rainbow went away. He was gone about half an hour. At the end of that time he returned with a large armful of hemlock branches suitable for making a broom.

"You must have had good luck," said Handie, when he saw him coming into the barn. "You have got back in very good season."

"Yes, sir," replied Rainbow, "I had very good luck indeed."

"Did you go to the woods beyond Mrs. Blooman's?" asked Handie.

"Yes," said Rainbow; "and I saw Mrs. Blooman herself—leastwise I suppose it was she."

"How did she look?" asked Handie.

"She looked pretty fierce," said Rainbow. "She came to the door to see me when I was going by."

"Did she speak to you?" asked Handie.

"Yes, sir," replied Rainbow. "She asked me who that was that had come into this house. I told her it was you. Then she asked me what you was going to do, and I told her you were going to put the house in repair."

"And what did she say to that?" asked Handie.

Handie pities her.

"She did not say any thing for a minute, but only looked at me pretty wild. Then she said she hoped you'd have a good time a doing of it; and so she turned round and went into the house, and slammed the door after her, and so I went on."

"Poor woman!" said Handie; "nobody likes her, and I suppose she knows it, and that makes her feel unhappy and cross. We'll watch for some opportunity to do her a kindness."

"Yes, sir," replied Rainbow, "so we will."

SURVEY OF THE FARM.   45

The garden.   Currant and gooseberry bushes.   Work enough.

CHAPTER V.

SURVEY OF THE FARM.

ON the evening of the first day after their arrival Handie and Rainbow set out just before sunset to walk about the farm. Behind the house there was a garden. There was a broken gate leading to this garden. Handie went in through this gate, and Rainbow followed him. The garden was pretty enough in itself, but it was very much neglected, and was filled with weeds, which were growing up, green and luxuriant, all over it. There were rows of currant bushes and gooseberry bushes against the fences on all the four sides of it; and here and there, in the different quarters, there were apple-trees and pear-trees, with a good many little apples and pears growing on them. In one corner of the garden was an old summer-house, all in ruins.

"Here is work enough for you to last a week," said Handie to Rainbow. "All these weeds must be pulled up and wheeled off into the barn-yard; and this summer-house is not

worth repairing. You will have to take it to
pieces, knock the nails out, and put the old
boards and pieces of joist on the wood-pile."

Along one side of the garden was a green
lane, with a sort of cart-path in the middle of
it, which led to pastures and fields that belonged to the farm, and that lay beyond the garden. Handie looked over the garden fence
into this lane. The grass on each side of the
roadway was all overgrown with brakes and
bushes, and hummocks of weeds.

"We'll grub up all those bushes and weeds,"
said Handie, "and then we will plow up the
whole lane, and harrow it smooth and level,
and then sow grass and clover seed over the
whole. In that way the ground will not only
look prettier, but it will produce a great deal
of good grass for the horses and cows to eat."

Handie then went along a little farther to a
place where the garden fence was broken down,
and there he passed through the gap into the
lane.

"Let us go down the lane," said he, "and see
what we come to."

So he and Rainbow went on down the lane.
There were fields on each side of it. One of
these fields was a mowing field, and the grass
in it was quite high.

"There'll be some grass to cut in that field pretty soon," said Handie. "Let me see."

So saying, he advanced toward the margin of the field, and, looking over the fence. took a survey of it.

"There may be five acres in that field," said he; "*four* or five. It is a pretty large field. I should think there might be three fourths of a ton or a ton to the acre. I can sell it standing to somebody in the village, and it will produce ten or twelve dollars. That's worth saving. Mr. James will be glad to hear of that."

"Shall you send that money to Mr. James?" asked Rainbow.

"I shall not actually send him the money," replied Handie, "but I shall report the amount to him, and give him credit for it. In that way, you see, it will go toward paying me for my work, and save his paying me other money, and that will increase the amount in his hands to be paid to me by-and-by. So, you see, I shall get it all myself sooner or later."

He then walked on down the lane. At the end of it he came to a pair of bars. These bars were put up well and strong, which rather surprised both Handie and Rainbow. It was evident that something had been done to them recently, for the top bar, which was broken, was

48 THE THREE PINES.

Fence mended.　　　　The pasture.　　　　Glimpse of the pines.

held up by two stakes driven crosswise into the ground, one on each side of the broken bar, and these stakes seemed to have been recently put there.

"Somebody has been mending up these bars," said Rainbow.

"Yes," replied Handie; "I wonder what it means."

Handie and Rainbow climbed over the bars and found themselves in what was evidently the pasture. It was an uneven piece of ground, with little hills and valleys all over it, and many groups of trees and bushes. They followed the fence along on one side, and found it mended in several places just as the bars had been.

"Somebody has certainly been patching up this fence," said Handie. "I don't see who it can be."

After walking along a little farther, Handie, looking through a little dell or valley which opened off to the right, obtained a view of the tops of some large pine-trees, with a glimpse of water beneath and beyond them.

"Ah!" said he, "these must be the three pines. Let's go and see them."

So he turned off immediately through the opening in the direction toward the trees.

As he and Rainbow approached the trees

THE THREE PINES.

they found that they were immensely large, and that the branches spread very wide on every side. The ground beneath them, and for a little distance all around, was smooth, and level, and very green.

There was a black colt, full grown, but looking very shaggy and wild, feeding near the trees as Handie and Rainbow approached them. When he saw Handie and Rainbow he pricked up his ears, held his head up high, and gazed at the new-comers a moment very earnestly; then wheeling suddenly round, he flung his heels up high into the air, and galloped away.

"I wonder whose colt that can be that has got into my pasture?" said Handie.

"There is an old man out here a fishing," said Rainbow; "we can ask him. There is a boy there too."

So saying, Rainbow pointed beyond the trees to a place where an old man was sitting upon some rocks by the shore of the stream, engaged apparently in fishing. There was a small boy near who seemed to be busy about the hooks and lines.

The fact was that the old man was blind, and the boy was baiting his hook for him. The old man had lived in the village a great many years, and was known to almost every body by the name of Old Uncle Giles. The boy, however, called him grandfather. The boy's name was Jerry.

"Jerry," says the old man, "I hear somebody coming. Who is it?"

"Wait a minute till I get this hook baited," said Jerry, "and then I'll look."

After having finished baiting his hook, Jerry looked up.

"I don't know who they are, grandfather," said he, after gazing at Handie and Rainbow a moment intently. "One of them is a black fellow."

"Call him a colored fellow, Jerry," said the old man. "They all like to be called colored people, and not black people. Every man has a right to be called by whatever name he likes best himself."

"But this is a boy," replied Jerry.

"The same rule holds good in respect to boys," added the old man. "Never call a boy by any name you think he don't like; it only makes ill blood."

By this time Handie and Rainbow had approached the place where old Uncle Giles and Jerry were stationed, and Handie bade them good-evening. The old man said good-evening in return, while Jerry contented himself with merely responding to the salutation by a nod.*

Handie stopped to have some conversation with the old man. He found that he was entirely blind, and that he was fishing by feeling alone. He *could* bait his hook himself and take off the fish, but it was more convenient for him to let Jerry do those things for him. As to the rest, throwing his line into the water, feeling the bite, and drawing up the fish, he could do all that, he said, as well as any body.

"These are fine old pines," said Handie; "they must have been growing here a great many years."

"Yes," replied the old man. "I can tell you almost to a day how old they are. Let us see: thirty and forty-five are seventy-five, and five are eighty. Seventy-five—yes, they are just about seventy-five or seventy-six years old."

"How do you happen to know their age so exactly?" asked Handie.

"Why, you see, I have heard old Squire Truro tell about them, and about how they were planted by his little Jinney," replied Uncle Giles. "He came to settle here in the year seventy, when he was about twenty-five years old. He had a young wife with him and this

* See Frontispiece.

little Jinney, who was then about four or five
years old. He bought this lot, and began to
clear the land to make his farm. He held the
farm afterward a great many years, and when
he died it fell to Jinney. But she was married
away to the westward somewhere, and her hus-
band was no farmer, and so she sold the farm;
and finally it came into the hands of a man by
the name of Eli Level, who lived here a while,
and then went away and let his farm out at the
halves, and so it got all run down, as you see.
But he has died lately, I'm told, and has left
the farm to a nephew of his."

"Yes," said Handie, "I'm the very one."

"You *be?*" exclaimed Uncle Giles, with great
surprise. And he turned round toward Handie, and looked at him, as it were, earnestly and
long, with his sightless eyes.

"I am glad to see you," said he; "and I
hope you'll have better luck with your farm
than your uncle ever had."

"But about the trees," said Handie, remind-
ing Uncle Giles of his unfinished story.

"Ah! yes, about the trees," said the old man;
"I was forgetting about them. I have heard
old Squire Truro tell the story very often—
though it is not much of a story, after all—only
it was kind of curious. And I have heard Jin-

ney herself tell about it too. The last time she came to Southerton she came out here into the pasture to see the trees, and she had the ground smoothed all around them. You see how smooth and level it is."

"Yes, it is," said Handie. "And now about the story."

"Why, Squire Truro was then about twenty-five years old, and he had a wife—a smart, capable young woman, and she was very fond of him. He was the first settler that came into the town, and he had no neighbor within ten miles. He came in through the woods by the blazed trees.* He built a small log house on his lot. It was not where the present house stands, but in the orchard to the northward of it. He afterward built a better house there, with a cellar to it. You'll find the mark of the cellar there now, if you look, though there is nothing left of it but a hollow place in the ground, all grown over with grass."

"I will look for it some day," said Handie; "but now go on about Squire Truro."

"He got along very well for some weeks,"

* A blazed tree is a tree marked by the surveyors in their first survey of wild lands. The mark is made by chipping off a spot of the bark as big as two hands, on the side of the tree, about four feet from the ground.

56   THE THREE PINES.

Squire Truro's troubles.   Jinney.   In the woods.   Jinney's plays.

continued Uncle Giles, "but then his wife fell
sick and died, and immediately the poor man
was in great trouble. He had a great mind, he
said, to give up his farm and go off, and never
come into the town again. He would have
done so if it had not been for Jinney, who was
then only about four years old. But he felt
that he must take care of her, and he had no
other property but this piece of land, and so
he determined to work on for her sake. He
thought that if he could make a farm here it
would be a good home for her at some future
day.

"So he went on clearing his land, and, as
there was nobody to leave Jinney with at
home, he used to take her with him into the
woods while he was felling the trees. Besides,
he naturally felt lonesome after his wife died,
and he liked her company. She used to amuse
herself while he was chopping by finding pretty
places to sit on the mossy rocks, and playing
with the flowers that grew there. She used to
make little gardens, too, out of the soft earth,
where trees had been torn up by the roots.
Her father made her a little hoe and shovel to
work with.

"One day, while she was working at one of
her gardens, she called out to her father and

wanted to know what he was cutting the trees down *for.* 'They are very pretty trees, father,' said she, 'and they make it very cool and shady, and I don't see what you cut them all down for.' 'It is because they shade the ground, Jinney,' said he, 'and so keep the corn and wheat from growing. I am going to raise some corn and some wheat here after the trees are all cut down, and then we can have some meal and some flour, and so we can make nice bread and cakes for you to eat.'

"Jinney seemed satisfied with this answer, and went on working in her garden. Presently she called out to her father again, and when he looked to see what she wanted, he found that she was holding up a small pine-tree about a foot high, which she had pulled out from the loose earth about the roots of a fallen tree. 'Father,' says she, 'will such a little tree as this keep your wheat and corn from growing?' 'No,' says her father, 'I don't think it would.' 'Then,' says she, 'I mean to plant it in my garden.'

"So she planted the tree, and afterward she planted two others in two other gardens at a little distance from the first. She told her father that he must be careful of her little trees, and not cut his great ones down in such a way

as to fall upon them, and he said he would; so
he cut the great trees so as to make them fall
away from Jinney's little ones. He did this
only to please Jinney at the time, for he had no
idea that the little trees would live and grow.
Afterward, to please her still more, he drove
three stakes around each of the little trees to
prevent any mischief from befalling them. He
had no doubt but that the trees would die, but
then he thought that long before the time came
for burning his lot Jinney would have forgotten all about them, and so, if he amused her by
pretending to take care of them for the time
being, that would be all that would be necessary.

"But Jinney did not forget her trees. Indeed, her father's putting the stakes around
them helped to make her remember them.
Very often after this, when her father went to
work in the woods, she used to carry a tin dipper down and water them from the stream, and
after a while her father found that they were
likely to live and grow. Then he began to
take an interest in them himself, and Jinney
was so much pleased to see them grow that she
made him promise that they should not be cut
down, nor burned down either when he burned
the fallen trees which lay all over the ground.

So, when the time came for burning the lot, Mr. Truro drew all the branches and small trees away from the places where Jinney's trees were growing. All the great trees had been cut in such a way as to fall away from them of their own accord. Then, besides, to make it more sure that they should not be burned by the fire, he laid them down carefully, and covered them over with wet straw and sods just before he set his fire, and then, after the fire was over, he set them up again; so they lived, and, in the end, became great trees, as you see. Jinney was always very proud of them. The last time she was in town she came down here into the pasture to see them."

"She must be pretty old by this time," said Handie.

"She is getting along some in life," said Mr. Giles, "though she is not so old yet. She is not more than eighty, and I am eighty-five myself. But she is getting somewhat infirm."

Here the old man interrupted himself in his story by exclaiming, suddenly, in a low tone,

"Hush! not a word. There is something nibbling at my hook."

A moment afterward he pulled up his line, and brought it in through the air to the shore with a pretty good-sized fish glittering and wriggling at the end of it.

"Yes, grandfather," said Jerry, "you have caught another perch."

Jerry took the perch off the hook and put it in the basket, and then baited the hook again.

"It is a little handier for me, you see," said the old man, "to have Jerry take off the fish and bait the hook, when he is here, but I can do it myself about as well. I come down here and fish alone very often."

"How do you find the way?" asked Handie.

"The way?" repeated the old man; "there's no difficulty about finding the way. I could not lose it if I were to try. I have been running about over this farm for fifty years and more, and I know the way all about it as well as I do about my own face."

After some farther conversation of this sort with Uncle Giles, Handie and Rainbow bade him and Jerry good-by, and resumed their walk.

"If we get along well with our work," said Handie to Rainbow, as they went away, "and if every thing prospers, you shall come down here Saturday afternoon and see if you can catch some fish."

"That's exactly what I should like," said Rainbow.

CHAPTER VI.

MRS. BLOOMAN.

ONE morning, a few days after Handie and Rainbow commenced their work at The Three Pines, while Rainbow was at work digging post-holes for some posts which Handie was going to set for a new fence about the yard, he saw a small boy coming in by the great gate. The boy seemed to be about six or seven years old. He had no cap, and his hair, which was of a very light color, hung like a mass of tangled flax all over his head.

He walked along slowly and timidly toward the place where Rainbow was at work, and when he got pretty near he stopped, and said, speaking in a monotonous and mechanical tone, as if he were reciting a lesson,

"Please, ma'am wants you to lend her a saw."

Rainbow stopped from his work and looked at the boy, and the boy looked at him without speaking a word.

"A saw?" said Rainbow, at length.

"Yes, ma'am—yes, sir."

"Whose boy are you?" asked Rainbow.

The boy stared, but did not answer.

"It is one of Mrs. Blooman's boys, I verily believe," said Rainbow. "I'll go and tell Handie. He said he would look out for a chance to do Mrs. Blooman a favor, and here is one come to him all ready at hand."

So Rainbow went and told Handie, who was at work in the shop, that a boy was out there wanting to borrow a saw, and he believed that it was one of Mrs. Blooman's boys.

"I'll come and see," said Handie.

So Handie came out into the yard to speak to the boy.

"Who sent you to borrow the saw?" he asked.

The boy stared, but did not answer.

"Can't you tell me who sent you?" asked Handie.

"My ma'am," said the boy at length.

"And who is your ma'am?" asked Handie.

The boy stared at Handie, and looked bewildered and frightened, but did not answer.

"What is your name?" asked Handie.

"Tom," said the boy.

"And what is your mother's name?" asked Handie.

Tom did not answer. The fact was, he did not know of any other name for his mother but ma'am.

"Do you live in the next house out that way?" asked Handie, pointing at the same time in the direction of Mrs. Blooman's house.

"Yes," said the boy.

"What does your mother want the saw for?"

The boy hesitated for a moment, and then, speaking out in a blunt and rapid manner, as if words had been pent up, and had at length escaped by some sort of explosion, he said,

"To saw some old boards."

"She ought to have a wood-saw for that," said Handie. "Tell your mother that I have not got any wood-saw. I have not got any thing here but carpenter's saws. Can you remember that?"

"Yes," said the boy.

"Be sure to tell it to her right," said Handie. "My saws are carpenter's saws, and they are not the right kind to saw up old boards for firewood. She ought to have a wood-saw."

Tom, having received this message, and having stood a moment staring stupidly, first at Handie and then at Rainbow, as if he expected something more to be said to him, turned round and went away.

Rainbow was somewhat surprised at Handie's sending him away without a saw. It is true, he was well aware that it was against all rule to use a carpenter's saw for sawing up old boards, which, if they did not contain old broken nails, were sure to be filled with sand and other gritty particles, by which the saw would certainly be dulled, but then he knew that Handie could sharpen his saw again without much difficulty if it did get dulled, and, as he had expressed a desire to find an opportunity to do Mrs. Blooman a favor, he thought that he would have been disposed to comply with this request, even if it did occasion him some trouble. Handie seems to have imagined that Rainbow was entertaining some thoughts of this kind, for as soon as the boy was gone he said,

"I don't know but that you think I ought to have lent her the saw, Rainbow."

"Why—no," said Rainbow, speaking, however, somewhat doubtfully; "she would have dulled it very much, I am sure, and it would have made you a great deal of trouble to have filed it again."

"I should have been very willing to take that trouble," said Handie, "if the thing itself had been right and proper for Mrs. Blooman to ask. We ought to be willing to take a great deal of trouble to do good to others, but it is not doing people good to humor them in unreasonable expectations. We must help our neighbors all we can, but we must not let them loll upon us and make us carry them, instead of doing what they can for themselves."

"That's so, I've no doubt," said Rainbow.

"It certainly is so," replied Handie; "and for a woman to want to borrow a carpenter's saw to saw up old stuff with for fire-wood, is going altogether too far. To humor her in such things as that would not be doing her any good. It would be doing her harm."

"I expect she will be put out about it," said Rainbow.

"Yes," replied Handie. "I have no doubt we shall have one or two good smart quarrels before she comes to understand what my principle is. But we shall be good friends in the end, you may depend."

Handie remained a few minutes longer with Rainbow to give him some farther directions about his work, and then, just as he was going away, he saw Tom coming in through the gate again.

He advanced slowly up toward the place where Handie and Rainbow were standing, and, when he was pretty near, he stopped and said,

E

"Please, ma'am says that'll do."

"That'll do?" repeated Handie. Then, turning to Rainbow, he said, "What do you suppose he means by that'll do?"

"Perhaps he means that a carpenter's saw will do for her to saw her boards with," said Rainbow.

"Yes," said the boy.

"It is possible, after all," said Handie, turning again to Rainbow, "that she may not want to saw up all the stuff for fire-wood, but only to cut an old board to a particular length for some sort of carpenter job. If that is what she wants, I would let you go and saw the board for her."

"I might go and see," said Rainbow.

"I wish you would," said Handie. "If she wants any small job of carpenter work done, tell her I will do it for her with great pleasure; but if she wants to saw up old stuff for fire-wood, tell her that I have no saws but carpenter's saws, and that it would spoil them, or, rather, that it would injure them very much to use them for such a purpose."

"Very well," said Rainbow, "I'll go. Come, Tom."

So, taking Tom with him, Rainbow went out of the yard, and walked along toward Mrs.

Blooman's house. On the way he endeavored to draw Tom into conversation, but without much success. When he reached the house he found Mrs. Blooman at the door, where she had taken her stand to await the return of her mes-senger, and learn what answer he would bring.

Rainbow, when he came near enough to speak, delivered his message.

While he was speaking, and after he had finished, Mrs. Blooman gazed at him steadily with a fierce and defiant look, and, after a short pause, during which she appeared to be en-deavoring to restrain a burst of passion, she finally seemed to give up the attempt, and broke out into a most violent fit of anger and vituperation. She called Handie and Rainbow all manner of hard names, and wound up by telling Rainbow himself never to dare to show his sooty face upon her premises again. "For if there is any thing in the world that I abso-lutely hate," she said, "it is a nigger."

So saying, she wheeled round and stalked off into the house, slamming the doors after her.

Rainbow, after waiting a moment to see if she would come back again, left the place, and returned to Handie to report the result of his mission.

"And, as soon as she said that," added Rainbow, in finishing his account of what occurred, "she turned about and went straight into the house."

"I am glad she went away without giving you any opportunity to answer her back," said Handie.

Rainbow did not reply.

"Though perhaps you would not have answered her back if you had had an opportunity," added Handie.

"I don't know," said Rainbow, looking thoughtful.

"The best thing to do when any body says any thing angry or cruel to us is not to make any reply, but to leave the sound of the angry words which they have spoken remaining in their ears, without doing any thing to disturb it. If we say any thing ourselves we take the sound away, whereas, if we leave it there for them to hear and think of, it makes them feel worse than any thing we can possibly say to pay them back."

"Yes," said Rainbow, "I think so."

"I presume that in a very few minutes after you came away, Mrs. Blooman, having nothing to think of but her own words, would gradually come to be ashamed of having spoken them, and very likely, if you had still been there, she would have said something to soften them a little. And now, very likely, the next time you see her she will be quite civil."

"Very likely," said Rainbow. "I don't care much whether she is or not."

The fact is that Rainbow was rather angry with Mrs. Blooman for having addressed him in so opprobrious a manner, and he had at this time very little inclination to make any effort to cultivate a good understanding with her in time to come.

CHAPTER VII.

LUCKY.

HANDIE, as it proved, was entirely correct in his idea of the effect which would be produced on Mrs. Blooman by having the sound of her own harsh and cruel words left upon her mind, with no reply from the injured person to turn her thoughts away from them or make her forget them. She went into the house muttering; but in a few minutes her anger against Rainbow, who, she reflected, was a mere bearer of a message, began to subside.

"I need not have scolded poor blacky so about it, after all," she said to herself. "It was not his fault, I suppose, that the young curmudgeon would not lend me a saw."

She accordingly determined that the next time she saw Rainbow she would try to make up with him.

One morning, a few days after the affair of the saw, while Rainbow was at work taking up the rose-bushes and other shrubbery in the front yard, in order to dig up the ground and set out the plants again in a more regular and

careful manner, he suddenly heard a loud out-
cry in the direction of Mrs. Blooman's house.
The sound was of some one crying,

"Ho! ho! Stop him! stop him!"

Rainbow dropped his spade and ran down
to the fence. He saw a black colt coming along
the road, followed by Mrs. Blooman, who seemed to wish to stop him. Rainbow at once rec-
ognized the colt as the one that he and Handie
had seen in the pasture. The colt came trotting along in the middle of the road, whisking
his tail and bearing his head very loftily, and
looking back now and then over his shoulder
to see how near his pursuer was. Finding that
she was at a safe distance, he turned to the side
of the road and began cropping the grass, still
walking along, however, as he did so, so as to
prevent Mrs. Blooman from getting any nearer
to him.

"Stop him!" cried out Mrs. Blooman when
she saw Rainbow. "Jump over the fence and
stop him! Do, for mercy's sake!"

Rainbow jumped over the fence, but the moment that the colt saw him he began to prance
and kick up his heels, and immediately he set
out upon the gallop, and went by down the
road in spite of all Rainbow's attempts to stop
him.

Immediately afterward Mrs. Blooman came up, out of breath, and her hair streaming in the wind.

"I'm *so* sorry he's got away!" said she.

"I'll go and catch him," said Rainbow.

"Oh, you can't catch him," said Mrs. Blooman. "It takes three men to catch him when he gets out in this way. It's of no use for you to try. And Joseph is away, and won't be back till noon, and before that time they'll have Lucky in the pound. They are all perfectly delighted when they get a chance to put Lucky in the pound, just to plague me. It costs me half a dollar to get him out again."

"Is his name Lucky?" asked Rainbow.

"Yes," said Mrs. Blooman; "and it is the wrong name for him altogether, for an unluckier beast than he is you never knew. He is always breaking out over fences and getting away, and he's harder to catch than a wild antelope."

"He'll make so much the better horse for all that life and spirit," said Rainbow.

"Yes," said Mrs. Blooman, "that's a comfort; but, in the mean time, he plagues me almost to death."

The fact was that Mrs. Blooman had herself taught Lucky a great many of his tricks by encouraging him to break over the fences into other people's pastures, and leaving him to get his living along the road-sides, until the people attempted to prevent it by putting him in the pound.

After some farther conversation, Rainbow said that perhaps he could catch Lucky, and even if he could not catch him he thought he could at least drive him home. At any rate, he said, he would go and try, if Mr. Level would spare him.

" I'll go and ask him," said he.

" Oh, it's of no use to go and ask him," replied Mrs. Blooman, in a despairing tone. "You may be sure he will not let you go."

" I'll go and see, at any rate," said Rainbow. So saying, he went up to the house and related the circumstances to Handie. Handie at once gave him permission to go after the colt.

"I have no idea that you can catch him," said Handie, "but perhaps you will be able to drive him home."

" I'll see what I can do," said Rainbow. " If I had some grain to give him, or something. Would it do for me to take a small piece of bread?"

Handie kept a supply of bread and cheese in one of the closets of his house to serve for lunch-

eons for himself and Rainbow. He told Rainbow that he might take as much bread as he
pleased.

So Rainbow took two pieces of bread, the remaining crusts of two loaves, and, putting them
in his pocket, he went out to where Mrs. Blooman was standing. He told her that Mr. Level
had said at once that he might go.

"I'll bring him back, if I can," said he; "and,
at any rate, I'll prevent his being driven to the
pound."

"I am very much obliged to you for going,"
said Mrs. Blooman; "but I don't think you can
do any thing with him at all, unless maybe to
drive him home, and then, very likely, he won't
come into the yard, but will gallop by and go
off the other way."

"We'll see," said Rainbow. "Good-by."

"Good-by," said Mrs. Blooman, "and good
luck."

Rainbow did not make any positive prom-
ises, but still he was very confident that he
should be able to catch Lucky, and that within
an hour Mrs. Blooman would see him riding
into her yard mounted on the colt's back. He
was well used to horses and colts of all kinds,
and knew exactly how to manage them. Horses
liked him too, and liked to have him manage

them, and almost always, however shy they may have been of other persons, when Rainbow came near them their shyness disappeared, and they became gentle and docile as lambs. There are many persons who have this mysterious influence over horses. Others possess it more particularly in respect to dogs. Whether it is that they have a particularly kind and gentle way, by which the animals are soothed and won, or whether they are marked by certain personal peculiarities, which the animals observe or feel by some hidden sense or faculty which we do not understand, is not quite clear. However this may be, it seems very certain that horses, dogs, oxen, birds, and even bees regard different persons approaching them in a very different light, and submit themselves to the influence and control of some much more readily than to others.

Rainbow walked quietly along the road, with his crusts of bread in his pocket; and, after going on until he arrived very nearly to the entrance of the village, he turned off into a side road, where he saw that the colt had gone.

This road was bordered by a wood on one side, and the back fences of a row of gardens belonging to the village houses on the other. Now and then Rainbow caught a glimpse of

Lucky feeding by the wayside at a little distance before him. The colt was evidently
watching him, for as he cropped the grass he
looked back frequently, and the moment that
he saw Rainbow coming into view he would
snatch a last mouthful hastily and walk on.

Rainbow advanced very slowly, keeping as
much out of sight as possible. As he walked
on in this way he drew a strong cord from
his pocket—for he always carried a supply of
strong strings with him, having learned from
experience that emergencies were continually
occurring in which some sort of cordage was
of great use. He now wanted to make a halter.

He knew very well how to make a halter
out of a cord. There was to be a piece to go
round the neck and tie, and a noose for the
nose. There were also to be two side pieces to
go down the cheeks, from the neck piece to the
noose, and also a long end to lead by. Rainbow fashioned all these parts very neatly, walking backward very slowly while he was doing
it, so that Lucky might not see what he was
about. If a horse or colt that you wish to
catch sees any thing like a bridle, or even a
cord in your hands, it makes him more shy than
ever.

When Rainbow had finished his halter he

put it in his pocket, and went and sat down upon a stone by the side of the road.

Lucky had been watching him all this time; but he now ceased to feel much uneasiness about him, for, having seen that his back was turned toward him, he supposed that it was some person going the other way. Still, he went slowly along the road, cropping the grass from the banks on each side by the way, and internally resolving that the moment that Mrs. Blooman or any of her emissaries came in sight, he would set off upon the gallop, and not stop till he had left them at least half a mile behind.

Lucky thought it prudent to keep a little watch upon Rainbow, but he did not feel much uneasiness about him, for he did not recognize him as one of the persons who had been sent to catch him on former occasions. So he went on cropping the grass quite at his ease, only looking back now and then, and taking care that Rainbow did not come too near.

Rainbow and the colt advanced in this manner by a slow progress, until at length they came to a place where a broad stream of comparatively smooth and still water ran along by the side of the road. The banks of the stream were covered with trees and bushes, except for a certain distance opposite to the road, where the ground had been cleared and sloped gradually down to the water, in order to afford a good opportunity for people riding by on horseback or in wagons to drive down to the water's edge and let their horses drink. Lucky, when he saw the water, thought he would go down and take a little drink. He was not particularly thirsty, it is true, but then the place looked so inviting that he thought he would go and taste of the water, though it was as much in play as any thing else.

He accordingly walked down to the edge, and put his mouth to the water, turning his head a little to one side as he did so, in order to keep an eye on Rainbow.

In the mean time Rainbow stopped in the woods on one side of the road, and, breaking off a number of small branches from the bushes there, he tied them up in his pocket-handkerchief so as to make a bundle such as a traveler, walking along the road, might be supposed to have to contain his clothes. He also cut a stick of the size and length of a walking-stick, and, putting one end of the stick through the knot of his bundle, he swung the bundle over his shoulder, and then, after remaining a few minutes out of sight in the woods, he at length sallied forth, and went walking along the road in a careless and unconcerned manner, whistling as he went, as if to beguile the time.

Lucky looked round and gazed for a moment very earnestly at Rainbow, but soon seemed to make up his mind that he was merely a wayfaring man accidentally passing that way, and that he had nothing to fear from him. After taking as much water as he wanted, he strolled along into the edge of the woods, and began browsing upon the leaves of the trees and bushes. Rainbow passed beyond him, without, however, appearing to take any notice of him, and then went down himself to the margin of the water; and after standing there a few moments, he sauntered along in a bold, but yet in a careless manner toward the edge of the woods where Lucky was browsing. Lucky, when he saw him coming, moved off a few steps, but Rainbow took no notice of him. He advanced to a large flat stone which was lying •upon the ground there, took his bundle off his stick and laid it down on the stone, and then sat down himself as if he were a traveler stopping by the wayside to rest.

"Now, Lucky," said Rainbow, turning toward the colt, and addressing him precisely as if he thought he could hear and understand, "it is of no use for you to play shy, for you are bound to be caught, and that before long. You only hinder my work a little more by holding out in this way, without doing yourself any good.

"Besides, you'll like me, Lucky, I'm sure, as soon as you get acquainted with me a little. I am a great favorite with all such touch-a-go skipper-jacks as you; and, though I am pretty steady myself, still, the wilder they are the better they seem to like me. Come, now, Lucky, walk up here like a sensible fellow, and let me see how my new halter will fit you."

Lucky seemed to pay very little attention to this address. He pricked up his ears when he heard Rainbow talk to him, but went on cropping the grass upon a little green bank at his feet, feeling apparently very much at his ease.

Just at this time Rainbow heard the voices of some boys that seemed to be coming along the road. The boys stopped when they came opposite to the place where Rainbow was sitting, and looked at him a moment, apparently with some surprise. They, however, said nothing, and Rainbow did not think it worth while for him to speak to them.

At length one of the boys happened to see Lucky, and immediately he called out to the rest,

LUCKY. 81.

They spy Lucky.   Rainbow claims ownership.   The boys puzzled.

"I say, boys, look there! There is Ma'am Blooman's colt got out again. Let's drive him to the pound. We can have some fun a chasing of him."

"No," said Rainbow.

"No?" repeated the boy. "Why not?"

"Because I've got the charge of him," said Rainbow. "I've come to catch him."

"That makes no difference," said the boy.

"Yes, indeed," said Rainbow, "it makes a great deal of difference. You can't drive a horse to pound while he is under any body's charge."

Rainbow was not much of a lawyer, it is true, but he thought it *ought to be* the law that an animal could not be impounded merely because he was astray, so long as he was still under the watch and care of some one sent by the owner to catch him and bring him back, and so he concluded that that was the law.

"Do you think that's so?" said the boy, turning round to his companions. He seemed to address this question to a quiet-looking boy, somewhat older than the rest, who stood a little apart.

"Is it, Jokky?" said he.

Jokky nodded, but did not speak.

"Very well," said the boy, "then we'll go on. We'll leave you the colt, snowball," he

F

82   THE THREE PINES.

The boys go on.   Help offered.   Rainbow tries the bread.   The rock.

added, addressing Rainbow, "and I hope you
will have a good time catching him."

So the boys began to move on. The one
whom his comrade had called Jokky turned as
he was going away and said to Rainbow,

"Do you want us to help you catch him?"

"No, I thank you," said Rainbow. "I think
I can catch him alone."

So all the boys went away.

The effect of the coming of the boys was at
first to alarm Lucky a little, but as soon as they
were gone he seemed to be entirely relieved of
all fear, and paid less attention to Rainbow's
presence than ever. Accordingly, in a few
minutes, Rainbow took one of the pieces of
bread out of his pocket, broke off a small portion from one end of it, and threw it out upon
the grass near the place where Lucky was feeding. Lucky smelled of it, and then with his
upper lip drew it into his mouth and ate it,
looking up, at the same time, to Rainbow, who
remained all the time sitting quietly upon the
rock, with an expression of surprise upon his
countenance, and a look, at the same time,
which seemed to say that he would like another piece very well, if Rainbow had another
piece to spare.

Rainbow waited a moment, holding another

piece all the time in his hand, in a position
where Lucky could see it. At length he tossed the second piece out upon the grass, as he
had done the first. Lucky seized it almost as
soon as it fell, and devoured it in an instant.
He then stopped eating the grass, and stood
looking earnestly toward Rainbow, as if waiting to see if any more was coming.

Rainbow held the remaining bread in his
hand so that Lucky could see it, and then very
deliberately broke off another piece. He did
not make Lucky wait very long; but when he
at length threw the piece, he threw it in such a
manner that the colt was obliged to step forward a little in order to reach it. By repeat-
ing this manœuvre he gradually enticed Lucky
up to the stone, and then he put down several
pieces, one after another, on the stone, and let
Lucky eat them. He kept talking to him all the
time, but he did not attempt to touch him.

"Now, Lucky," said he, "why can't you and
I be good friends at once, without any more
playing off and on?" Here he put down another small piece of bread upon the stone, and
Lucky ate it.

"I'm a colored boy, it is true, Lucky; but
then *you* can't complain of that, for you are
blacker than I am, and nobody likes you the

less on that account. I am not heavy to carry, and then I shall never whip you unless you really deserve it, and then, you know, it will be for your good."

Here Rainbow put down another piece of bread, and, while Lucky was eating it, he raised his hand a little and began very gently to stroke down and rub the colt's nose. Finding that Lucky seemed rather to like this rubbing, he gradually worked his hand up higher until he got it up to Lucky's forehead, which he rubbed and curried with his fingers for some time. He then took his hand away, and gave Lucky another piece of bread.

Lucky soon lost all the shyness which he had felt at first, and allowed Rainbow to rub his head all over just as he pleased. Rainbow continued to give him bread from time to time, and at length cautiously pulled the halter out of his pocket and put it on. He kept the cord as much as possible out of Lucky's sight, and continued rubbing him all the time that he was putting it on. In fact, Lucky had not the least idea what Rainbow was about until he was fully secured.

Lucky had never been broken to draw in harness, though he had often been saddled and bridled, and had carried persons on his back.

RAINBOW AND LUCKY.

He seems to submit.

Of course, now, as soon as he found that there was a halter on his head, although he could not understand how it was put on, he felt that he was captured, and he did not think of making any more resistance. He allowed Rainbow to lead him quietly out into the road.

88   THE THREE PINES.

Rainbow mounts.   No bits.   A run.   Lucky's observations.

CHAPTER VIII.

LUCKY BROUGHT HOME.

A S soon as Rainbow had brought Lucky to a smooth place, he turned him round, the ground being a little inclined, and placed him in such a manner that he himself, standing by his side, had the advantage of the rise, and then leaped upon his back. The colt immediately sprang forward, and set off along the road upon the full run, in the direction, of course, away from home. He knew that there were no bits in his mouth, and that the boy on his back, whoever he might be, had no means of controlling him, and so he concluded that, by suddenly springing into the road and galloping away in that manner, he might frighten him, and perhaps make him fall off.

Now a horse who is running can easily tell, by the posture which the rider assumes on his back and the motions that he makes, whether the rider is afraid, and is shrinking back, and wishing the horse to stop, or whether he feels at his ease and enjoys the motion. Lucky very soon perceived that the latter was the state of the case in respect to Rainbow. In fact, Rainbow felt perfectly at his ease. Nothing pleased him better than to be riding a horse at a full run. He leaned forward, and pressed his knees against the colt's sides, and shouted HEY—EY —EY! in such a manner as to convince Lucky at once that there was no hope of making him fall off.

In fact, perceiving this, Lucky changed his plan altogether, and now no longer desired to make him fall off. A horse likes to frighten a timid rider, and to get rid of him if he can ; but he loves a bold one, and would rather have him for his master than not.

Accordingly, when Lucky found that Rainbow was having such a good time in taking a ride, he began to take pleasure in it too, and, pretty soon coming to a place where the road was straight and level for about half a mile, he determined to let Rainbow see what he could do, and as soon as he had fairly entered upon this straight and level reach, he put himself at the very top of his speed, and flew over the ground for the whole half mile like the wind, Rainbow cheering and encouraging him by his voice and by the pressure of his knees all the way.

At length, finding that he was getting a little out of breath, Lucky began to slacken his speed; but Rainbow, instead of appearing to be glad to have him stop, was only the more eager to urge him on. He leaned forward still farther in his seat, and pressed his heels against the colt's sides, as if he were spurring him, and continued shouting to him, as if to encourage him to gallop on. Lucky was thus fully convinced that it was useless to attempt to frighten Rainbow by running away with him, and so he gradually relaxed his speed, and finally fell into a walk. He then walked out to the side of the road, and began cropping the grass there as quietly as if nothing had happened.

Rainbow dismounted, and stood by Lucky's side a moment, patting his head and neck while he was eating.

"I told you you would like me, Lucky," said he, "and you did not believe me."

Here Rainbow patted Lucky's neck more, while Lucky himself went on eating quite at his ease.

"And now, Lucky," said Rainbow, "as I have not any bridle or bits to guide you with, you must come with me to the woods and let me cut a switch. I shall pat you on the cheeks with this switch to make you go one way or the other, but you need not be afraid. I shall not hurt you. It will only be for a sign to let you know which way I want you to go."

So saying, Rainbow led the colt to the roadside at a place where trees and bushes were growing, and there, while he held him with the halter wound round his arm, he cut a small switch. He then led Lucky out into the road again, turned his head toward home, and mounted him. Lucky began immediately to travel along the road in a very quiet and regular manner.

Whenever he evinced any disposition to go to the side of the road in order to get some more grass, Rainbow patted him on the side of the head so as to drive him back into the road again, and if he went too far, then he patted him on the other side of the head, and so kept him right. Lucky soon learned to understand this system, so that a very slight touch was sufficient to indicate to him that he was to turn a little, and thus Rainbow could guide him at his pleasure, though he had no bit or bridle.

He went on in this way until he came to The Three Pines. There he turned in, though he had some difficulty in making Lucky understand that he wished him to go there; for Lucky, though he knew the pasture at The

Three Pines well enough, had not been accustomed to call at the house.

Rainbow rode up into the yard. Handie was at work in the shop planing a board. His face was turned toward the window. When he saw Rainbow coming he paused from his work, but remained in the same position, with his hand upon the plane.

"I have got him," said Rainbow.

"Yes," said Handie, "I knew you would get him, but I did not think that you would be quite so quick about it."

"I'll go with him to Mrs. Blooman's," said he, "and then I will come right back."

"Very well," said Handie; "only stop and talk with the lady a few minutes if you have a good opportunity, and get a little acquainted with her."

So Rainbow, patting the colt on one of his cheeks, turned him round and guided him home. Mrs. Blooman was at the door when he entered the yard. She clapped her hands together and looked extremely pleased.

"I am *so* glad!" said she. "How *did* you manage to catch him?"

"Oh, there's no difficulty in catching him," said Rainbow. "He is one of the nicest colts that ever I saw."

So saying, Rainbow dismounted from the colt, and walked up with him toward the door, with the end of the halter in his hand. Tommy stood on the step of the door near his mother, looking on with eyes very large and round.

"And now," said Mrs. Blooman, "I must pay you something for catching the colt, for you have done me a great service."

"Oh no, ma'am," said Rainbow, "there is nothing to pay. It is a pleasure to go and catch such a colt as that."

"Then I am very much obliged to you, I am sure," said Mrs. Blooman.

"You are not obliged to me at all," said Rainbow, "but to Mr. Level, if to any body, for it was his time that I took, and not mine."

"Then I am very much obliged to him," said Mrs. Blooman, "and I wish you would tell him so."

"And shall I put the colt in your field?" said Rainbow.

"Yes, if you will be so good," replied Mrs. Blooman.

"But first let me give Tommy a ride round the yard on his back," said Rainbow.

"Oh no!" exclaimed Mrs. Blooman; "I should be afraid."

94   THE THREE PINES.

Mrs. Blooman consents.   Lucky taken to pasture.   The kitchen.

" Yes, mother, yes," said Tommy, speaking
in a whining and supplicating tone.

" There's no danger," said Rainbow, " the
colt is so gentle. Besides, I will lead him by
the halter."

Mrs. Blooman at length reluctantly consented that Tommy might ride, and so Rainbow,
bringing Lucky up close to the steps, jumped
Tommy upon his back, and then gave him a
ride two or three times round the yard. Then
he led him to the bars and turned him in to
Mrs. Blooman's field. The field was adjoining
Handie's pasture. The fence between the field
and the pasture was broken down in several
places, but on the other sides of the field it was
kept in pretty good repair.

When Rainbow came back from turning out
the horse, Mrs. Blooman called to him from the
door and asked him to come into the house a
minute. So he went in. He was surprised to
find how neat and tidy every thing looked in
the little kitchen to which Mrs. Blooman conducted him. She gave him a seat by a table
near a window, and said that she was going to
bring him a piece of pie ; so she went into the
pantry, and, taking an apple-pie down from a
shelf, she cut out a large slice for him. When
she had cut into the pie once from the circum-

ference to the centre, and then was placing her knife again, measuring with her eye the proper distance for a good generous slice, the thought of the rude and cruel manner in which she had spoken to Rainbow when he came to see about the saw occurred to her mind, and she immediately moved the knife along several degrees on the edge of the plate, so as to make the slice larger still.

Rainbow found that the pie was excellent. He was surprised at this too, and it was very natural that he should be so, for when we find that a person is marked with bad or disagreeable qualities of one kind, we are very apt to form an unfavorable opinion of him in all respects. But when we do this we usually make a great mistake, for good and bad qualities are mixed together in almost all human characters, and nothing is more common than for a woman who is rude and selfish, and makes herself hateful to all who know her by her ugly temper and her perpetual scolding, to be very neat in her housekeeping, and an excellent cook.

While Rainbow was eating his pie, Mrs. Blooman asked him where he got the halter that he used to bring Lucky home with. Rainbow said that he made it out of a cord that he had in his pocket. Mrs. Blooman asked him if he was willing to give it to her.

"It would not be good for any thing for you," said Rainbow, "for you could not tie Lucky up with it. He would break it in a moment. But if you have got a piece of rope I can make you a good strong one some evening when my work is done."

Mrs. Blooman said that she had not any rope except her clothes-line, but she could cut a piece off from that. Rainbow, after looking at the clothes-line, said it would do very well, and so Mrs. Blooman cut him off a piece of it as long as he required for his halter.*

When Rainbow returned home he related to Handie all that had occurred, and then went back to his work, secretly hoping, it must be confessed, that before many days Lucky would contrive to get away again.

* A few evenings after this Rainbow made a very neat halter from this rope by means of a wooden marline-spike that Handie made him out of a piece of oak wood, to do the splicing with.

Next house.   Front yard.   Back yard.

CHAPTER IX.

MRS. FINE.

THE next house to the farm of The Three Pines, on the side toward the village—that is, in the opposite direction from Mrs. Blooman's, was a neat, pretty one-storied dwelling, where lived a very polite and smooth-spoken lady whose name was Mrs. Fine. The house was, in fact, on the confines of the village itself. The sidewalk of the village began there, with young trees on the outer margin of it. There was a front yard before the house, with shrubbery planted along the fence, and a straight walk, paved with brick, which led from the gate to the front door. This walk was bordered on each side with long and narrow beds of flowers.

By the side of the house was a passage-way leading to a back yard, where there was a barn and a shed. Behind the barn was a small garden.

Mrs. Fine was a very different woman from Mrs. Blooman. She was very gentle and affa-

G

ble in her manners, but she was quite artful and designing, and she generally attempted to ac-complish her ends by some sort of adroit man-agement and manœuvring.   .

It happened one day, when Rainbow was going into the village on an errand for Handie, that Mrs. Fine was quite in a state of perplex-ity just before Rainbow had passed her house. The difficulty was that she wished to go away in the wagon, and there was no man about the house to harness the wagon. The horse was in the barn, and the wagon was under the shed, but the man was gone away, and she was quite perplexed to find out some way of getting the horse harnessed. She thought of sending to some one of the neighbors, and was trying to think to which one to send, when, as she hap-pened to look out at the end window, she saw Rainbow coming along.

"Ah!" said she, "here comes young Mr. Level's colored boy. I think I can manage so as to get him to harness the wagon for me."

She immediately went out at the front door of her house, and walked down the little path which led through the yard to the front gate, as if accidentally, and stood there until Rainbow came along.

"Good-morning, Rainbow," said she, speaking in a very bland and polite manner. "What a pleasant morning it is!"

"Yes, ma'am," said Rainbow, "it is very pleasant."

"And how does Mr. Level get along with his work?" asked Mrs. Fine.

"Very well, I believe," said Rainbow.

"I saw, when I went by the other day, that you had been putting the borders of the shrubbery in order in the yard, and I want you to come in here and look at some flowers that I have got. Perhaps Mr. Level would like to have some of the same kind."

Rainbow was quite unwilling to stop. Still, he could not very well refuse such an invitation, so he went into the yard. Mrs. Fine talked with him a minute or two about the flowers, and then told him that she understood he was very fond of horses, and asked him to go with her through a little gate which led into the back yard, and so into the barn, and look at her horse. Rainbow said that he could not stop very well then, as he was on his way into the village on an errand for Mr. Level; but Mrs. Fine told him that it would not detain him but a moment, and, besides, he could go into the street almost as near that way as by going back through the front yard again.

So Mrs. Fine led Rainbow into the barn. The horse was in the stall. He laid his ears back and looked round in a surly manner when he heard persons coming.

"He does not seem to be very good-natured," said Rainbow.

"No," replied Mrs. Fine, "he is not very good-natured—at least, he is not very gentle. I don't think he means any thing by it; but he is so full of life and spirit that we are afraid to harness him, though I can drive him well enough when he is harnessed. But I suppose you would not be afraid of him?"

"No," said Rainbow, "I should not."

"Now I think of it," said Mrs. Fine, "I want to go away in the wagon this morning, and our man is not at home. And since you are here, if you would be good enough to bridle the horse and lead him out for me, I should be very much obliged to you."

"Certainly, ma'am," said Rainbow, "I'll do that." So he walked at once into the stall, commanding the horse in an authoritative voice, as he did so, to "stand round." The horse knew at once from Rainbow's tone and manner that he was a person whom horses were accustomed to obey, so he submitted at once. Rainbow bridled him and led him out.

"And now," said Mrs. Fine, "I don't know that I can put the collar on alone. If you would be good enough to put the collar on and to crupper him, perhaps I could make out to do the rest."

"If you wish to have the horse harnessed, ma'am, I can harness him for you just as well as not," said Rainbow. "If you had told me so at the gate, I should have been perfectly willing to come and do it."

"I should be *so* much obliged if you would," said Mrs. Fine.

So Rainbow harnessed the horse into the wagon, and then tied him to a post in the yard, which Mrs. Fine pointed out to him. Mrs. Fine then told him that she was very much obliged to him indeed. He had taken a great deal of trouble, she said, and he could not tell how great a favor he had done her. She hoped that some day or other she should be able to do something for him. She supposed he was not hungry, it was so near breakfast-time. If it had not been for that, she said, she would have given him a cake.

When Rainbow went home that day and related to Handie how Mrs. Fine had manœuvred to get him to harness the horse, Handie laughed very heartily, but Rainbow himself seemed

102   THE THREE PINES.

Mrs. Blooman and Mrs. Fine.   Management of the children.

to feel great contempt for such an indirect and roundabout mode of management in accomplishing one's ends. He liked Mrs. Blooman, after all, he said, a great deal better than Mrs. Fine, for she, although she was a little rough and plain-spoken, was at least honest, and meant what she said.

I think that Rainbow's judgment in respect to Mrs. Fine was, on the whole, very correct. Her poor children often had rather an uncomfortable time of it on account of her not being open and honest with them. She would put but very little butter on their bread, for example, spreading it extremely thin, and then pretend that she had put on a great deal. The children could have borne very well the having but little butter, but it was very vexatious, when there really was so little, to have their mother pretend that there was a great deal. And then, what, in fact, made it a great deal worse, she always required them to admit that it was a great deal.

Her management was pretty much the same in every thing. One day she promised them that if they would put the yard in order, and sweep it clean, she would give them a nice drink of molasses and water.

Now the children were very fond of molasses

and water, but then they liked it sweet. So Billy asked his mother how much molasses she would put into it.

"Oh, I can't say exactly how much I will put in," said Mrs. Fine, "but I will make it very sweet and good."

So the children put the yard in order, and swept the paths very clean. While they were doing it their mother went to the molasses jug, and, finding that there was not much molasses in it, she poured in some water, and then, shaking the jug, she mixed the two components well, thus very much increasing the quantity, and, at the same time, greatly deteriorating the quality of the saccharine compound.*

Then, when the children had finished their work, she poured out some of the diluted molasses from the jug into their two mugs, and then showed it to them before she poured the water in.

* Saccharine means sweet, in the sense of sugary. Some persons might ask why, if saccharine means sweet, we can not always say sweet at once, and so not have to use the word saccharine at all. The reason is that the word sweet has several different senses, and the word saccharine applies only to one of them. Thus we sometimes say that a rose is sweet, but can not say it is saccharine, because the sweetness of it is not sugary. On the other hand, we can say that the juice of a corn-stalk is saccharine, because the sweetness of it is of a sugary nature.

"See!" said she; "see how much molasses I am giving you. The bottoms of the mugs are covered very deep."

Then, when she had filled the mugs up with water, and given them to the children, she stood by to see them drink it, and to make them say that it was very sweet.

"Is it not sweet and good?" said she, when Billy had drunk his portion.

Billy looked not very well satisfied, and said, in a quiet way, as he put down the mug,

" Not *very*."

"Not very? Oh, Billy, how can you say so, when I took so much pains to make it sweet for you? I am sure that Luny will not be so ungrateful."

So Luny, who had tasted of her drink, and discovered what the state of the case was, in order not to be forced to give a distinct answer, said that she was not going to drink hers just then, and so put it down until her mother went away.

Whenever Mrs. Fine had any thing irksome or disagreeable for the children to do, she would almost always contrive to represent it in the light of a gratification to them. For instance, one morning she told Billy that she would like to have him make haste and "do up his chores," because she was going to let him have a nice run into the village when he got through. So Billy made haste with his work, and, after he had finished it, he went to his mother, cap in hand, and said,

"Mother, it is all done. May I go now?"

"Yes," said his mother, "in one minute. Wait till I get the pail."

"The pail?" repeated Billy, inquiringly.

"I want you to take a pail with you," said his mother, "and get me a little meal at the store. You can take the pail with you, you know, just as well as not."

So Billy's mother gave him what she called the pail, but which proved to be a heavy bucket, and told him that he was to get it filled with meal and then bring it home, and she charged him not to stop either going or coming, as she was in a hurry for the meal to make some bread.

Thus the nice little run into the village turned out to be only an errand, with a heavy load to carry each way.

CHAPTER X.

A NEW PLAN.

HANDIE formed a more favorable opinion of Mrs. Blooman from the report which Rainbow brought back in respect to her kind treatment of him on the day when he caught the colt for her than he had previously entertained. He was particularly struck with Rainbow's account of the neatness of her house and of the excellence of her cooking, so far as he had an opportunity to judge of it from the taste of the pie.

" So you liked the piece of pie that she gave you ?" said Handie.

" Yes," replied Rainbow, " it was very nice. In fact, it was very nice *indeed.*"

Rainbow smiled as he said this, and nodded his head with a look of great satisfaction.

" And the house looked neat inside ?" continued Handie.

" It was as neat and tidy as a pin," said Rainbow.

" I have been thinking," said Handie, " that

perhaps it would be a good plan to make a bargain with her to board us; it would be so much more convenient than for us to go to the tavern in the village."

" I think it would be an excellent plan," said Rainbow—" a *very* excellent plan."

" Then," said Handie, " I'll go and see what she says about it."

Handie, soon after this, went to Mrs. Blooman's to propose the plan to her of taking him and Rainbow to board. Mrs. Blooman, when she saw him coming, met him at the door with a scowling and defiant look, presuming that he had come to complain of something—of Lucky's breaking into his pasture perhaps, or of the hens coming continually into the garden. The visits which her neighbors paid to her were generally prompted by some such considerations as those. Handie, however, was not discouraged, and, after holding some little conversation at the door, Mrs. Blooman invited him in.

Handie went in and took his seat by the window, where he saw a vacant chair. Mrs. Blooman followed him in, but did not take a seat. She stood near the fireplace, looking at Handie in a suspicious and half-angry manner, as if she was awaiting an attack from him.

"This is a very pretty room," said Handie, looking about him. It was, indeed, quite a pretty room.

"Pretty enough," replied Mrs. Blooman, moodily.

"And how nice you keep it!" said Handie.

"There's no reason why people should live like pigs, if they *are* poor," said Mrs. Blooman.

Mrs. Blooman began to be a little softened by the compliments which Handie paid to her room and to her housekeeping, and she felt her feelings of reserve and defiance all at once giving way. But the thought immediately came to her mind that probably Handie had some covert design in saying these smooth things to her, and she determined not to be taken in by any such flattery. So she drew herself up again, looking sterner than ever, and said,

"I suppose you have come with some sort of complaint or other, Mr. Level, and you may as well out with it first as last."

"Oh no, Mrs. Blooman," replied Handie, "I have no complaint to make at all. What should I have to complain of?"

"I expected you had something of that sort to say," rejoined Mrs. Blooman. "People are always blaming me for something or another. Nobody never comes to see me unless they have some complaint to make or some fault to find."

"You must say nobody *ever* comes," said Handie, looking up with a good-natured smile. " It is not good grammar to say nobody never."

"Oh, never you mind my grammar," said Mrs. Blooman ; " I don't pretend to talk correctly. I could not if I should try. All I care for is to have people understand what I say."

" They do," said Handie. " Rainbow says that that is one thing he likes you for particularly—that you say just what you mean, and so he knows just how to take you."

Mrs. Blooman's countenance relaxed quite into the semblance of a smile at hearing this. She was pleased to hear thus, at second-hand, of any body's liking her for any thing. A compliment that you hear at second-hand always gives you more pleasure than one that is paid you directly.

" I am very far from having any complaint to make against you," continued Handie. " Indeed, the only thing almost in which we have had any thing to do with you as a neighbor was your rewarding Rainbow so generously for catching Lucky the other day. I am sure that whenever I come to live here in my house I shall like you for a neighbor very much—

though I suppose that long before that time
you will be gone away."

" Gone away !" repeated Mrs. Blooman;
" where should I be gone to ?"

" Oh, I don't know," replied Handie. "You
will be married, and be gone off somewhere."

" Nonsense !" exclaimed Mrs. Blooman.

" It is not nonsense at all," said Handie. " A
woman as young and good-looking, and as capable as you, does not remain very long un-
married."

" Oh, Mr. Level !" exclaimed Mrs. Blooman,
" what a flatterer you are."

" No," replied Handie, " I am not a flatterer.
I am not old enough to be married myself, it is
true, but I know pretty well how the men
think about these things. I am sure that there
is great danger that before I come to live on
my farm you will be married and will be gone
away. There is only one thing in the way,
and that is that you are so very capable, and
so perfectly able to take care of yourself."

" Why, Mr. Level, you don't think that is
any fault, do you ?" said Mrs. Blooman.

" No," replied Handie, " not exactly. It is
not a fault, certainly ; and yet men are very apt
to think so when they are looking out for a
wife. You see, when a man looks out for a

wife, he wants somebody to *take care of*, not somebody to take care of him. He likes to have his wife a little timid and gentle, so that she will lean upon him, and look to him for help and for protection. When a woman shows that she is perfectly able to go alone, and fight her own way through the world, he lets her go. He wants one who will lean upon him, and look to him, and let him fight for her."

Mrs. Blooman cast her eyes down, and looked somewhat embarrassed, but did not reply.

"But now," said Handie, "let me tell you what my object is in coming to see you this morning. I don't think you could ever guess."

"I'll tell you what I did guess," replied Mrs. Blooman, "when I saw you coming."

Mrs. Blooman then went on to say that she supposed he was of course coming to find fault about something or other, but she could not tell what it was that he was going to complain of, unless it was of Lucky's getting into his pasture so much.

Handie replied to this that he knew very well that Lucky liked to come into his pasture pretty well, but he did not blame him at all for that, he said, for the feed was very good in the pasture, and the fences were very much down.

"But then," said Handie, "we will arrange

all that by-and-by. When I get the fences put up, I will make a bargain with you, and take Lucky into my pasture for so much a week. It won't be a great deal, and then, by means of the other part of the plan which I have to propose to you, it will be very easy for you to pay."

Handie then went on to propose that Mrs. Blooman should take him and Rainbow to board. They would come to her house every day for their meals, or she might send the food over to them, whichever she preferred. Mrs. Blooman was much surprised at this proposal; but, after some hesitation, she consented, and the bargain was made. She preferred that they should come to her house, and Handie said that he should prefer that plan too. The price to be paid was agreed upon; and it was settled, moreover, that when the fences were put up, Lucky was to be taken into the pasture regularly, and a certain sum—I believe it was twenty-five cents a week—was to be deducted on his account from the price which Handie was to pay for his and Rainbow's board.

CHAPTER XI.

AT MRS. BLOOMAN'S.

THE plan which Handie arranged with Mrs. Blooman for boarding himself and Rainbow was carried into effect, and it was found to work well, and much to the satisfaction of all parties. It had the effect, too, of producing quite an improvement in Mrs. Blooman's appearance and manner. Handie and Rainbow took pains always to arrange their dress neatly when they went to their meals, and this tended to make Mrs. Blooman more careful about her dress and appearance. Then Handie encouraged this tendency by noticing and remarking upon her dress when he found that any thing which she had put on was prettier, or nicer, or fitted better than usual. This is the true way to promote improvement in those who, though within the reach of our influence, are not in any sense under our control. It is not by pointing out their faults and exhorting them to amend, but by noticing what is right, and commending it, and thus encouraging them to love and to

H

cultivate the virtue, whatever it is that you
wish them to acquire.

Handie and Rainbow made a great improvement in the outward appearance of Mrs. Blooman's house, and of the yards about it, while
they boarded there. They did this gradually
and insensibly, mending a gate one day, and a
piece of the fence the next, and so on. Mrs.
Blooman soon began to take a great interest
herself in these changes. Sometimes Rainbow
would come over to the house fifteen or twen-
ty minutes before it was time for supper, and
spend the time which he had to spare in mending something, or putting things in order. In
such cases he would always employ Tommy to
help him. And then, after supper, when he
went away, he always left a little work for
Tommy to do by himself, and then remembered always to take notice of it the next morning, and to praise Tommy if the work was well
done.

Sometimes Tommy came over to Handie's
house, and then Rainbow would set him at
work there at picking up chips, or carrying off
shavings and piling them up in a great heap in
the garden, where they were to be burned.

While Rainbow was boarding at Mrs. Blooman's he cultivated his acquaintance with Lucky

in a very successful manner. He used to save all the little crusts and ends of bread, and other such things that came into his hands, and put them in a little box which he kept upon a beam in the shed, and then, whenever he had occasion to go near the field where Lucky was pasturing, or whenever he had a few minutes leisure after dinner or tea, he would take some of them in his hand to give to Lucky. Indeed, he made it a rule never to go within sight of the colt without having something in his hand or in his pocket to give him to eat.

The consequence was, that whenever Lucky saw Rainbow coming he knew that he was going to have something good to eat, and he used to come at once from whatever part of the field he might be in to the bars, or to the place at the fence where he saw Rainbow standing. And, after a time, when the arrangement was finally made for putting Lucky into Handie's pasture, Lucky would always look up whenever he saw any body coming into the pasture to see whether it was Rainbow or not. If the person coming had a white face, Lucky, after gazing a moment, would turn away very much disappointed, and with as great an expression of contempt upon his countenance as the face of a horse is capable of assuming, and go on feeding upon the grass. But if he saw that the face was black, he knew at once that it was Rainbow that was coming, and he would immediately abandon the grass which he had been eating, however rich and green it might be, and set off at once at full speed, trotting or cantering over the undulations of the ground that intervened, and leaping over all the obstacles that came in his way, until he arrived at the place where Rainbow was, when he was sure to receive his expected reward.

Whenever Mrs. Blooman wished Lucky to be caught, Rainbow was always very much pleased if Handie would allow him to go and catch him. He generally took no bridle, nor even a halter, in such cases, but when he had called the colt to him and had given him his crusts of bread, he would mount upon his back and ride home without saddle or bridle. He could guide the horse in such cases by patting his cheeks with a switch, in the manner already described, and when he had no switch he would lean forward and do it with his hand.

Rainbow *could* ride upon Lucky standing up. In such cases he used to take off his shoes and stand barefoot on Lucky's back over his hips. He held on by a long sort of bridle

RAINBOW'S HORSEMANSHIP.

which he made for this purpose out of a cord. In this way he used to ride round and round the yard, greatly to the delight of Tommy, who always looked on while Rainbow was performing this feat with eyes full of wonder and admiration.

120   THE THREE PINES.

Digging stones.   Rainbow coming home.   Some cause of excitement.

CHAPTER XII.

THE TWO ROBINS.

ONE afternoon, about sunset, when Rainbow had been at work in the pasture digging flat stones for Handie to use in mending the cellar wall at a place where it had caved in, Handie came to the door of the room which he used for a shop, and looked down the lane which led along the side of the garden to see if Rainbow was coming.

"He was to leave off his work before sunset," said Handie to himself, " and it is time for him to be here.

"Ah! here he comes," added Handie, a moment later.

He saw Rainbow as he spoke just coming along the lane. He had his crowbar in one hand, and the shovel with which he had been digging in the other. He stopped after he got through the bars and looked back, and his countenance denoted that he was excited, and much displeased at something which had occurred.

Handie turned his eyes in the direction toward which Rainbow was looking, and he saw a boy coming along with a gun in his hands.

"What's the matter?" said Handie, calling to Rainbow.

"Why, here's a great ugly fellow who has been shooting my two robins."

"Your two robins?" repeated Handie, not exactly understanding.

"Yes," replied Rainbow. "I had two robins that had a nest in one of the pines, and he has been shooting them."

"Has he shot them both?" asked Handie.

"Yes," said Rainbow; "they were both standing together on a stone. They had been playing about there with each other, and that fellow watched his chance and shot them both at one fire. I saw him just before he fired, and hallooed out to him, but it was too late. Cruel fellow! If I had had another gun I would have shot *him*."

"Oh no, Rainbow," said Handie.

"I would," said Rainbow; "that is, if the gun had been loaded with salt, I would have shot the salt into his legs."

"Do you think that salting his legs would be the way to cure him of his cruelty?" asked Handie.

122   THE THREE PINES.

Boy with the gun.   Remedy wanted.   Alger.   His triumph.

"It would have punished him for it, at any rate," said Rainbow.

By this time the boy with the gun arrived at the bars. He had the two dead birds in his hand. Rainbow, in the mean time, had come on some way from the bars toward Handie.

"Here he comes now," said Rainbow.

"Yes," said Handie; "and I am glad you have not shot him in the legs."

"Then I wish you would contrive some better way to cure him," said Rainbow.

"I will try," said Handie.

The boy was walking along from the bars toward the road. Handie knew him. He was a boy named Alger. He lived near the middle of the village.

Alger diverged from his way so as to come a little nearer to Handie as he passed along toward the road, and when he was pretty near he held up the two birds and said,

"See! Two birds! I killed them both at one shot."

"That was a good shot," said Handie.

"Yes," said Alger, "I think it was."

"A skillful shot, I mean," said Handie; "not good in any other sense."

"Why not?" asked Alger.

"Because Rainbow says they were a father

and mother bird," repeated Handie, " and that they had a nest in one of the great pines."

" Perhaps there were no young ones in it," suggested the boy.

" Yes there were," said Rainbow. " There were two; I saw them."

" How could you see them?" asked Alger. "The nest is out at the end of a very high bough. You could not get at it."

" I climbed up above it," said Rainbow, "and looked down."

" Then perhaps the birds have flown away by this time," said Alger.

" No," replied Rainbow, " for I saw them only yesterday, and they were not more than half fledged."

" Then I don't know what they will do," said the boy, thoughtfully.

" Could not you get the nest down, Alger," said Handie, " and take care of the little birds? Now you have killed their father and mother, the least you can do is to take care of the young ones."

" Oh, I could not get them," replied Alger. " The nest is out at the end of a long, slender branch, away up almost to the top of the tree. I might perhaps shake the nest off, but it would kill the little birds to fall all the way to the ground from so high."

"Then they will have to stay there and starve, I am afraid," said Handie.

"*I* could get the nest down, I think," said Rainbow, "if I had somebody to help me."

"Should you be willing to help him, Alger?" asked Handie.

"Yes," said Alger, " I'll help him, but I know he can't do it."

"And would you lend me a hand-saw?" asked Rainbow, turning to Handie.

Handie replied that he would, and Rainbow ran off to get a saw. He returned pretty soon with a saw in his hand, and also a coil of small rope, which he brought from somewhere in the shed. He called Alger to follow him, and immediately set off toward the lane. Alger put his gun into the entry of the house, laying down the birds by the side of it, and then set off to follow Rainbow.

"I know it is of no use," said he, "but I'll go."

So the two boys walked along together back toward the pasture.

Rainbow's feeling of indignation against Alger for having shot the birds was somewhat softened by Alger's readiness to go with him and help him make an attempt to rescue the young ones. He, however, was not in a very amiable mood toward his new companion after all, and he walked along silently.

"Let me carry the rope," said Alger.

"No, thank you," said Rainbow, "I can carry it."

"But you've got the saw," said Alger.

"I can carry the rope and the saw both," said Rainbow.

When, at length, they arrived at the foot of the tree on which the nest was built, Rainbow looked up and presently obtained a view of the nest.

"There it is!" said he, pointing up into the tree.

The nest was very high up in the tree, and, what was worse, it was built near the very end of one of the longest branches, where it would have been wholly impossible for man or boy to get near it.

"Yes," said Alger, "there it is, true enough, and there it will stay. You can't possibly get it."

"I'll try," said Rainbow.

Rainbow put his saw down by the side of the tree, and then throwing the rope, which was coiled in a small coil, down upon the ground, he began coiling it again in a larger coil. When the new coil was completed he put it over his head, placing it in such a manner that a part of the coil rested upon his neck and shoulders, and the rest hung down before him.

"There!" said he; "now I can climb the tree and take the rope up with me."

"And how about the saw?" asked Alger.

"I can take that up in my hand," said Rainbow; "and I want you to come up after me."

So saying, Rainbow began to climb up into the tree, and Alger followed him. The lower branches were at some little distance from the ground, but Rainbow succeeded in getting up to them without much difficulty, and then, reaching down his hand to Alger, he helped to pull him up. The two boys then went on ascending, by means of the branches, until they reached the level of the branch that the nest was built upon. The nest was out near the end of the branch, very much farther out than it would be safe for any boy to go.

"There's the nest," said Alger. "Now how are you going to get it?"

"Perhaps I can't get it at all," said Rainbow; "but we will see."

So saying, Rainbow looked up above the place where he was standing, and selected a good stout limb which grew out from the tree

above the one on which the nest was built. He
climbed up to this upper limb, and fastened
one end of his rope to it. While he was doing
this he had given the saw to Alger to hold.
When he came down again, he went as far as
he could on the limbs below and around the
one that contained the nest, and then tied the
lower end of the rope to that limb, as far out
as he could reach, in such a manner as that
when he should have sawed off the limb, at a
place farther in toward the tree, the rope would
help him hold the part that was sawed off, and
aid him in drawing it in toward him, until he
could reach the nest.

This plan he now proceeded to put into exe-
cution, and it succeeded very well. He held
the end of the branch with one hand, between
the place where he was going to saw it and the
place where the rope was tied, and then, with
the other hand, he proceeded to saw it off. Alger sat on a stout limb near by, close to the
place where it came out from the tree, and
watched the operation.

The limb which Rainbow was sawing off,
though not large enough to bear the weight of
a boy beyond the place where he was sawing
it, was still pretty long and heavy, but the rope
supported it so much that Rainbow had noth-

ing to do but to hold and steady the inner end with his left hand, while he worked the saw with his right. As soon as the separation was effected, Rainbow handed the saw to Alger to hold, while he drew the bough carefully in. As he drew the end in toward him he saw that the two little birds were safe in the nest, and this made him more careful in his movements than ever.

"You'll get them," said Alger—"I verily believe you'll get them! Poor little things! If I had known that there were young ones in the nest, I would not have shot the old birds."

As soon as Rainbow brought the end of the limb in near enough to reach the nest, he took the nest carefully off, and handed it to Alger.

"There!" said he. "Hold them carefully now, while I untie the cord."

Accordingly, while Alger held the nest and the saw, Rainbow untied his cord from both the limbs to which it had been attached, and then, after having coiled it up in a short coil, he threw it out from him clear of all the branches of the tree, so that it might fall to the ground. He threw the branch down too. He and Alger then came down themselves, bringing with them the saw and the nest with the two little birds in it. The birds kept opening

The birds.

their mouths all the way. They were, in fact, wholly unconscious of the great change which was taking place in their condition and prospects, and thought of nothing but of the old birds coming to give them something to eat.

I

130 THE THREE PINES.

Alger carries the nest.   Way to kill young birds.

CHAPTER XIII.
BLACK CAT.

A LGER was very earnest to carry the nest himself in returning from the pasture to the house, and Rainbow allowed him to do so. He watched the little birds all the way, and seemed to pity them, and before he reached the house he began to feel quite interested in them. He named one of them Chick, and the other Chiggery.

On the way along the lane he proposed to stop and give them something to eat.

But Rainbow said no. That's the way, he said, that boys always kill the young birds that they try to bring up, by giving them a great deal too much to eat.

"Why, these birds are very hungry," said Alger. "Don't you see how they keep open-ing their mouths?"

"Oh, that's only a way they have," said Rain-bow; "they don't mean any thing by it. Birds always open their mouths for a great deal more than is good for them."

When at length the two boys arrived at the house, Rainbow found that Handie had gone to supper. He was strongly inclined to keep the little birds, and to take care of them himself; but Alger was so desirous of having them that he yielded, and allowed Alger to take them away.

Alger was at first somewhat at a loss to know how to dispose of all that he had to carry. There were the nest with the two living birds, and also the two dead birds and the gun.

" I can tie the legs of the two birds together with a string," said Alger, " and so hang them across the gun."

" You had better not let the little ones see them there," said Rainbow. " It will break their hearts to see their father and mother hanging dead across the very gun that killed them."

" Then I will put them in my pocket," said Alger.

So he put the two dead birds in his pocket, and, taking the nest with the two living birds in it in one hand, and holding the gun over his shoulder with the other, he turned toward the road.

" Take good care of them," said Rainbow, as Alger began to walk·away.

132   THE THREE PINES.

Rainbow's Instructions.   Mrs. Fine.   Her questions.   Her politeness.

" Yes," said Alger, " I will."

" And don't give them too much to eat," added Rainbow.

" No," said Alger, " I'll be careful."

Rainbow, after watching Alger until he had got out into the road, went to put the saw and the rope away, and then set off to go to Mrs. Blooman's to supper.

When Alger, on his way home, reached Mrs. Fine's house, Mrs. Fine, as it happened, was out in her front yard, looking at her flowers. She happened to be near the gate when Alger was going by, and, observing that he had something in his hands, she stopped to see what it was.

" What pretty little birds !" she said, when she saw them; " and what a pretty nest they are in !   Where did you get them ?"

" We got them off of one of the three big pines."

" We ?" repeated Mrs. Fine : " who do you mean by *we?*   Who was there besides you ?"

" Rainbow," replied Alger.

" Mr. Level's black boy ?" said Mrs. Fine.

" Yes," replied Alger.   " The nest was out on the end of a limb, and he climbed up and sawed off the limb."

" What a smart fellow he is !" said Mrs. Fine; " and what pretty little birds !"

"Yes," replied Alger, "he is a very smart fellow indeed."

So saying, Alger went on. Just at that moment, however, little Billy happened to come to one of the parlor windows, and, observing that his mother was looking at something which Alger had in his hand, he ran out to see what it was. He did not get to the gate, however, until Alger was gone. He immediately wanted to open the gate and run after him, or at least to call him back, but his mother was afraid to have him do so, because Alger had a gun, and she was afraid that Billy might come to some harm by it.

"What is it, mother?" said he, eagerly. "What has Alger got? I want to see."

"Oh, it's nothing," said his mother; "at least, nothing worth seeing."

"But he had a nest," said Billy, "and I believe there were some little birds in it."

"Yes," replied Mrs. Fine, "but they were ugly little things. There were scarcely any feathers on them."

"But I want to see them," said Billy.

"Oh, they were not worth seeing at all," said Mrs. Fine; "they were as ugly as little toads. That black boy that lives at Mr. Level's got them, and he is a very wicked boy for doing it.

I should not wish to see them at all, if I were you."

As she said this, Mrs. Fine held the gate so as to prevent Billy from going out until Alger had got too far away to be called back. Billy fretted and whined, and seemed very much disappointed; but at length his mother tried to quiet him by saying that she had got something very pretty indeed to show him up by the house. He finally allowed himself to be led away from the gate, though he went muttering, and saying that he did not believe his mother had any thing at all to show him. She, however, said positively that she had, and finally she showed him a flower, such as he had seen a hundred times before, and which she only showed him now, under a pretense that it was something curious and pretty, in order to divert his attention from Alger and the nest.

In the mean time Alger went home with his two birds.

"I mean to take good care of them," said he, "until they grow up; and as I shall feed them every day with my own hands, they will grow up to know me, and be very tame. I will make a cage for them. I can make it myself out of a box, by putting in wires for the front of it. I'll have one of the wires made so as to take in and out, for a door. There is no hurry about the cage, for it will be some time before the birds will be old enough to fly; but I will look up the box as soon as I get home, and I'll put the wires in the first afternoon that I have time."

With these reflections and plans occupying his mind, Alger arrived at the house where he lived. As he entered the yard, his little brother Georgie and his sister Ann came running to see what he had got. He held the nest up high to prevent their seizing hold of it in their eagerness, and they, reaching up, took hold of his arm to pull it down.

"Let us see!" said they. "Let us see!"

"No, no," said Alger. "No, no. Let go of my arm! let go! There are two little birds in the nest, and you will kill them."

"Let us see the little birds," said the children. "Hold them down and let us see them."

Alger promised to let the children see the birds presently, when he got to the steps, if they would let him alone till then, and promise not to touch them.

The children were very ready to promise, and so Alger went on till he reached the steps, and there, after putting his gun in the entry of the house, he sat down upon the steps, and

showed Chick and Chiggery, as he called them,
to the two children. The children were greatly
delighted at the sight of the birds, and they
were .quite still while they looked at them,
Alger having told them that if they made much
noise they would frighten the poor little things.
Alger did not tell the children any thing about
his having shot the old birds, and his having
brought them home in his pocket, but simply
said that the reason why he brought the nest
home was that the old birds had "got killed,"
and there was nobody to take care of the young
ones.

After allowing the children to look at the
little birds a few minutes, Alger said it was
time for him to go and find a box to make a
cage for them; so he rose from his seat on the
steps, and went, with the nest in his hand, out
toward the barn. The children followed him.
When Alger got into the barn he looked for a
place on a beam where he could put the nest
for safety while he was finding a box. The
children wished him to give them the nest to
hold, or, at least, to put it in some low place
where they could watch it; but Alger thought
it not safe to trust them, and so he put it up
out of their reach, and then sent them out of the
barn.

Plan for the cage.   The nest put in the box.   Feeding the birds.

"When I have got the box," said he, "and am ready to put the birds in, I will let you see them again."

Alger soon found a box which he thought would answer his purpose very well. It was a box that was made to contain candles, and it was very nice and clean. It had no top, but this Alger thought was of no consequence, for he was intending to make the top the front of the cage, and to close it with the wires which were to form the bars. Alger carried the box out into the barn, and placed it in a sort of manger which was not used, and then put the nest into it in one corner. The children stood by while he did it.

When the nest was safely bestowed in this place, Alger fed the birds. He fed them cautiously, as Rainbow had recommended. In fact, he did not give them half as much as they seemed to want. The children begged him to give them more, but he would not.

At length, after the feeding was completed, Alger took the children with him and went out, shutting the door carefully behind him.

"They are too little," said he to himself, as he went away, "to get out of their nest to-night, and to-morrow I'll make the cage.

"On the whole," said he, "I believe I'll go

and find the wire, and cut it up in proper lengths for the bars to-night, so as to be all ready to put the bars in to-morrow morning."

He accordingly went to find the wire, and in about fifteen minutes he came back to the barn in order to measure the open side of the box for the purpose of ascertaining the proper length for the bars. Just as he opened the door and stepped into the barn, he saw a large black cat rush out from the stall where he had left the box, and dart rapidly down through an opening in the floor which led under the barn. Alger saw that she had something in her mouth. In a state of great alarm, he hurried to the manger where he had left the box. The box was there, but the nest was gone. He found it a moment afterward, bottom side up, on the floor. By the side of it was the head and the little claws of one of the birds. In a word, the cat had eaten Chick, and run away with Chiggery.

Alger was very much troubled at this spectacle, and for a few moments he did not know what to do. Finally, perceiving that the mischief which was done was wholly irreparable, he took up the nest and the remains of the little bird from the floor, and carried them down to the foot of the garden, and threw them away as far as he could throw them into the bushes.

He took the old birds out of his pocket too, and disposed of them the same way. He then returned slowly home, greatly dejected and depressed in spirits at the thought of his having been the means of bringing such complete and total destruction upon the charming little family which two hours before were living so innocently and so happily together in their peaceful and secluded home on the great pine.

" At any rate," said he to himself, " whatever else I shoot, I'll never shoot a robin again."

Thus, although Handie's mode of managing the case proved unhappily unsuccessful, so far as saving the lives of the little birds was concerned, it had the effect of awakening the dormant sentiments of humanity in Alger's bosom, and in this manner the operation of it, as a moral remedy for Alger's hardness of heart, was attended with much more favorable results than could have been expected to follow from any such process as that which Rainbow was disposed to resort to of shooting salt into his legs.

140   THE THREE PINES.

The boys' opinion of Rainbow.   Rainbow's kindness.

CHAPTER XIV.

RAINBOW'S PARTY.

ALTHOUGH, when Rainbow first arrived in the town of Southerton, the boys were disposed to look upon him with dislike and aversion, they soon changed their minds in respect to him. Whenever he found any of them in any perplexity or trouble, he was always ready to help them, and inasmuch as, in respect to ingenuity and address, as well as personal strength, he was far superior to most of them, he was often able to do for them what they were wholly unable to do for themselves. He used to save long, slender strips of pine wood from Handie's work for them to make kites of, and climb up into trees to release their kites when they became entangled there, and give them shavings to make bonfires of, and cut and shape canes and fishing-poles for them in the pasture, and put hooks upon their fishing-lines, and let them ride upon Lucky, and do them a thousand other similar favors.

One afternoon, when Rainbow was at work

in the yard, he saw three small boys standing together at the gate and looking in. They seemed as if they wished to come in, but were afraid. Two of them were apparently endeavoring to induce the third, who was the smallest of the three, to go forward.

At length the small boy seemed to consent, and began to come forward, though with a timid air. He wore a straw hat, with the brim on one side entirely worn away. He came up to Rainbow, the two others following him at a little distance, and when he was near enough to be heard, he said,

" Give us some shavings, please."

"Some shavings?" said Rainbow, looking up from his work. " What do you want the shavings for?"

" To make a bonfire," said the boy.

" Yes," said Rainbow, " I'll give you some shavings. But where are you going to make your fire?"

" Out in the road," said the boy.

" No," replied Rainbow, " that will not do. If you make a fire in the road it will frighten the horses when they go by. I will give you a place to make the fire out in our garden."

So Rainbow gave each of the three boys as many shavings as he could take up in his arms, and then led the way into the garden, the boys following him, each with his arms clasped around such a mass of shavings that he could scarcely see which way to go. Rainbow conducted them to the centre of the garden, where there was a considerable open space at a point where all the principal paths met, and there the boys put the shavings down and made a great heap of them. Rainbow then gave them two matches apiece to kindle their fire with, and left them in order to go back to his work.

"The boys like so well to see the shavings burn," said he to himself, as he walked along, "that I have a great mind to make a large bonfire for them in the evening some time. A bonfire in the evening would make a fine show."

On farther reflection, Rainbow determined to carry this plan into effect. It was Tuesday when he first conceived of the idea, and from that time during all the rest of the week he saved all the shavings that were made, instead of burning them, as he had been accustomed to do every two days in the garden.

The next Monday was the day that he fixed upon for his bonfire, and he gave out the invitations to the boys to come on the Saturday previous. Indeed, he fixed upon Monday for the day on account of the convenience of having Saturday as the day for giving the invitations, for he usually saw a great many of the boys on Saturday afternoon.

He did not tell the boys when he invited them that he was going to make a bonfire, but only that he was going to have a party, and that he wanted them to come. He said that they were to come at five o'clock and to stay till half past eight, so that they would all be at home at nine. He not only invited those that he happened to see, but he sent word by them to others whom he thought he might not see, and he gave them all authority to bring with them any others that they thought would like to come. The only restriction was that nobody was to be invited who was over twelve years of age.

"You see, we don't want any very big boys to come," said he, "because they can't play so well."

"No," said one of the little boys in reply. "And, besides, they run against us so hard, and pull us about, and plague us."

Every boy was to bring a piece of bread and butter for his supper.

"Because, you see," said Rainbow, "we shall want some supper, and Mr. Level and I have not our oven ready to bake in yet. Take a

144   THE THREE PINES.

Mode of packing.   Handie makes a contribution.   The boys assemble.

large slice of bread, and when you have but-
tered it, cut it in two exactly in the middle, and
double one half over upon the other half, and
then wrap it up in a piece of paper."

Rainbow had not intended to provide any
entertainment himself for his party except the
bonfire and plays, but to have the guests depend entirely for their supper on the bread and
butter which they should bring in accordance
with the directions above referred to.   But
Handie, when he came to understand the par-
ticulars of the plan for the party, for Rainbow
had taken care to ask for his approval of it before he took any steps toward carrying it into
effect, determined to add something on his part
to the supplies which the boys might bring.
Accordingly, on Monday noon, he sent Rainbow into the village to buy three sheets of
freshly-baked gingerbread, which contained
eight cakes each, and, as Rainbow said that
the number of boys that he expected would not
exceed ten or twelve, the three sheets would
supply them with two cakes apiece, which Handie advised Rainbow to give to them after they
had eaten their bread and butter.

The boys began to come before five o'clock,
each with his paper parcel in his hand.   As
fast as they came, Rainbow conducted them to

a cupboard in the kitchen of the house, where they could deposit their parcels.

"We will keep the supper here," said he, "until the time comes to eat. Each of you must remember how your parcel looks, and what shelf you put it upon."

When all the boys had assembled, Rainbow told them that he was going to have a bonfire as soon as it was dark, and that the place where it was going to be was down in the pasture.

"Because," said he, "the light of the fire will be a great deal prettier shining among the trees. And now," he added, "the first thing is to move the shavings out to the place where we are going to have the fire."

"Well," said the boys, "have you got a wheelbarrow?"

"We could not carry enough in a wheel-barrow," said Rainbow. "I have got a better plan than that. Come and see."

So Rainbow led the way out to a place in the yard where there was a great heap of shavings lying against the house, under a window where he had thrown them out. By the side of the shavings was a heap of hemlock boughs, which Rainbow had brought there that day.

"Now, boys," said he, "we have got to make all these shavings up into a big ball."

K

So saying, Rainbow produced a rope, the same which he had used in sawing off the limb of the pine-tree when he took the birds' nest down. This rope he laid at length upon the ground, and then placed four of the hemlock boughs, side by side, across it. These boughs being, as hemlock boughs always are, very flat, though very branching, covered the ground with a sort of net-work of twigs, well adapted to hold the shavings.

"Now, boys," said he, "pile the shavings on this flooring that I have laid for them."

The boys immediately went to work, taking up the shavings by armfuls and putting them upon the hemlock boughs, until almost the whole pile was transferred to the new place. Then Rainbow took the two ends of the rope and brought them up on each side, putting in, at the same time, new boughs at the sides and end, and winding the rope round and round, and turning the mass of shavings over and over, as he did so, until he formed it into an immense ball.

"Now, boys," said he, when at length the work was completed, "roll this ball along the lane to the pasture."

So the boys immediately began to roll the ball along. Some pushed against it with their

THE BIG BALL.

hands; others took long sticks and poles which
they found in the yard, and, running them under the ball, pried with them. In this way
they soon rolled the great ball across the yard
to the bars which led to the lane, and thence
through the lane till they came to a gate which
led to the pasture. One of the boys held this
gate open, while the others rolled the ball
through.

As soon as they entered the pasture they
came to a place where there was a long descent
in the road.

"Now, boys," said Rainbow, "here is a hill.
Give the ball a fair start, and it will roll down
the hill by itself, and save you the trouble of
pushing it."

So the boys went on with the ball to the
brow of the descent, and then, all giving it a
good push together, they set it a going down
the hill. It rolled on, going faster and faster
as it advanced, and bounding over the little
obstructions and inequalities of the ground
which it found in its way, until at length, near
the bottom of the slope, it came to a turn in
the path, and here it broke away from the path
altogether, and rolled off among the rocks and
bushes, where it was soon brought to a stop.
The boys all immediately began to run down

150   THE THREE PINES.

Joy of the boys.   Place of the bonfire.   Games.   The picnic.   Cool spring.

the hill after it at full speed, brandishing their poles, and filling the air with their shouts and peals of laughter.

They soon got the ball into the road again, and rolled it on to the place which Rainbow had selected for the bonfire. It was a place where there was a smooth and level plat of ground, with trees and bushes all around it. Here Rainbow untied the big bundle, and, taking off the hemlock branches, he left the shavings in a pile in the middle of the plat of ground. He laid the hemlock branches by themselves in a separate pile on one side.

"Now, boys," said he, when this had been done, "first we'll have supper, and then we'll play hide and go seek here among the bushes until it is dark enough to light the fire."

So the whole party returned to the house to get their stores of bread and butter. They went to the cupboard, and there each took his own parcel from the place where he had put it. Rainbow's parcel consisted of the sheets of gingerbread which he had previously placed on an upper shelf of the same cupboard. He also took with him a tin dipper, to get water for the boys to drink from a spring which issued from the ground under a cool, mossy rock near the place which he had selected for the bonfire.

Thus provided, they all went down the lane, talking and laughing together in a very merry way until they reached the ground.

When they came back to the place of the bonfire, Rainbow began to look about for a place where there were smooth, flat rocks for the boys to sit upon; and while they were rambling about among the bushes to find a suitable place, they came upon a cow feeding upon a green slope, with a little tinkling bell hanging to her neck.

"Ah!" said one of the boys, "here is a cow!"

"Is she cross?" asked another boy.

"No," said Rainbow, "she is not cross. It is Mrs. Blooman's cow; I know her very well. I drive her home every night."

"I wish we had some of her milk," said one of the boys, "to drink with our supper."

"Mrs. Blooman will let us have some," said Rainbow, "if I only had two boys here to run and ask her."

The boys seemed to shrink back from this commission. They all seemed afraid to go and ask Mrs. Blooman to give them any milk.

"Tommy," said Rainbow, turning to Tommy Blooman, who was there in the party with the rest of the boys, "you can *run*, can't you?"

"Yes," said Tommy, "I can run pretty fast."

"Then you may run home across the fields, and ask your mother if she will let us have some milk from her cow. Tell her I will keep the measure of all I take, and pay her. Who'll go with Tommy?"

"I! I! I'll go! Let me go!" cried all the boys. As soon as they found that Tommy was to take the responsibility of delivering the message, they were all ready to go. Rainbow appointed two to go with Tommy, and sent them off with their commission.

In a few minutes they returned with word from Mrs. Blooman that Rainbow might take as much milk as he wanted. So the boys all sat down on the rocks and ate their bread and butter, and then Rainbow divided the ginger-bread among them. While they were eating the gingerbread Rainbow milked his dipper full of milk four times from the cow, and so gave each one of them a good drink of milk. The boys all said that it was the best supper they had had for a long time.

After the supper the party played at hide and seek among the bushes for half an hour, until the sun had set and it began to grow a little dark, when Rainbow said it was time to

kindle the bonfire. Rainbow did not wait until it was *very* dark, for he did not wish to make
the boys late in getting home.

Rainbow appointed the youngest boy in the
party, who, as it happened, was Tommy himself, to set the pile of shavings on fire. He tied
a handful of shavings to the end of a long stick,
and then gave the boy a match to light them
with. The boy laid the stick down upon the
ground while he lighted his match and set fire
to the little bunch of shavings at the end of it.
Then he took the stick up, and reached it out
toward the pile of shavings in order to set the
whole heap on fire.

He was going to light the fire on the top,
but the boys called out to him to light it below.

"Set it afire at the bottom, Tommy," said
they—"at the bottom, so that it can burn up
through, and make a great smoke."

In compliance with this wish, Tommy lighted the fire at the bottom, and as soon as it began to blaze up pretty well on one side of the
heap, the other boys rolled the whole pile of
shavings over upon the burning part, so as to
cover it up entirely.

"Now you've put it out," said Tommy, in a
complaining tone.

Smoke.   Flashes of flame.   Dancing about the fire.   Hemlock boughs.

" No," said the boys. "See the smoke coming up through."

The smoke was indeed coming up through, and it came up faster and faster, until at length the whole top of the heap seemed full of rising fumes, which became every moment more and more abundant, and ascended in dense volumes into the air. In a few minutes flashes of flame began to break out among the rolling masses of smoke, and very soon the whole heap was in a blaze. The heat which the fire threw out became so great that the boys had to hold up their arms before their faces and eyes to screen them from it, and very soon they were obliged to fall back, or they would have been burned. The boys danced about the fire, waved their caps in the air, and made the whole place resound with their shouts and joyous outcries.

When the blaze began to subside a little, and while the heat of the fire was at its *maximum*—that is, at its greatest point, Rainbow called the boys to take the hemlock branches and put them on all together. Each boy was to take one branch from the heap, and, at the word of command, which Rainbow was to give, all were to put them on the fire. Such a crackling, and snapping, and such fierce shootings and burstings of flame as were produced when this was done was scarcely ever heard before.

The light of the bonfire shone on the foliage of the bushes and trees around it, and produced a very striking effect. The boys all said that they had never seen such a good bonfire before in all their lives.

After the bonfire had burned down, Rainbow gave all the boys a ride on Lucky, who, as it happened, was feeding in the pasture at that time, and who came readily when Rainbow called him, notwithstanding the presence of so many boys. Rainbow jumped the boys up upon the horse's back one after another, until there were four on at a time. He let the first four ride on for a little way through the pasture, and then, taking them down, he put up four more, and so on until all had had a ride. By this time they arrived at the gate of the pasture, where they had come through rolling the ball of shavings. Here Lucky was dismissed, and went back to his grass again; and the boys, with Rainbow at the head of them, walked along the lane till they reached the house, and then separating, they went by various ways to their several homes.

CHAPTER XV.

THE TORPEDOES.

WHILE Handie and Rainbow were together at The Three Pines, Handie set
apart an hour every evening for Rainbow to
spend in learning to write. Sometimes, on
these occasions, Rainbow wrote letters to his
mother; sometimes he copied accounts; and
sometimes he wrote out carefully, upon a small
piece of thick paper, some maxims of conduct,
or some important principle of moral duty,
either in prose or verse, which he afterward
adorned with an ornamental border, more or
less artistic, and then hung up on the walls of
his room.

One evening, not long after the bonfire,
Rainbow had for his writing-lesson the following lines, written by the poet Pope:

" Teach me to feel another's woe,
    To hide the fault I see :
  That mercy I to others show,
    That mercy show to me."

"That verse contains an excellent rule for us to follow," said Handie, "and so you had better copy it handsomely, and make a pretty border around it, and hang it up in your room."

"Must we always hide the faults we see?" asked Rainbow.

"Yes, always—unless there is some special good to be done by making them known," said Handie. "For instance, when you saw that man hiding away his carpet bag in the hay—what was his name?"

"Burkill," said Rainbow.

"Yes, Burkill," continued Handie. "When you saw him hiding away his carpet bag, and afterward knew from that that he had stolen the watch, you did right to make it known, in order that justice might be done. And sometimes there are other reasons for making known what people have done that is wrong. But, unless there is some special good reason for making them known, we ought to conceal the faults of other people as much as we can, and not go about publishing them to all the world. That is doing as we would be done by."

"Yes," said Rainbow, "I think it is."

I think myself that the principle which Handie thus enunciated to Rainbow is very correct, though sometimes, in practice, when we hap-

pen to know of some fault committed by another person, it is difficult to decide whether it
is our duty to make it known or to conceal it.
In such cases as that of Burkill and the stolen
watch, it is very clear that the wrong done
ought to be made known. On the other hand,
in respect to the ordinary faults and foibles of
our friends and acquaintances, it is plain that
we ought to do all in our power to conceal
them. They who take pleasure in talking over
these faults, and in setting them out in a strong
and ridiculous light among each other, merely
for amusement, evince a very unchristian and
a very hateful spirit, and do very wrong. But
then there is a third class of cases, in which a
conscientious person is sometimes quite at a
loss to know whether a certain act of wrong-
doing which has come to his knowledge ought
to be divulged or concealed.

A case of this kind occurred in Rainbow's
experience while he was at work with Handie
at The Three Pines. The circumstances were
as follows :

It seems that little Tommy Blooman, one
day when he was sent to the village of an errand by his mother, saw some boys firing torpedoes. Now a torpedo, as I suppose most of
the readers of this book are aware, is made, not

with gunpowder, which to be exploded must be touched by fire, but of what is called fulminating powder, a substance which is so extremely sensitive that it may be exploded almost by a touch. At any rate, a very little heat, such as is produced by friction or a smart blow, will set it off. The torpedoes are made by putting a little of this powder in a paper with sand and a leaden shot. Then, when you throw it down upon the ground or upon a floor, the very slight grinding motion which the shot produces among the particles of the sand explodes the fulminating powder, and makes quite a loud noise.

Now Tommy had never seen or heard of torpedoes until the day when he saw the boys firing them in the village. The boys had just come to the end of firing them for that time when Tommy came by, and were about to go home. He heard one or two go off, however, and was very much excited by the noise which they made. He asked the boys to fire some more, but they said they could not fire any more then, for it was time for them to go home. Then he asked them to give him some of the torpedoes; so one of the boys gave him two, and Tommy put them in his pocket.

Now Tommy had no idea how the torpedoes

were to be fired, but he supposed that, like India crackers, they were to be touched off in some way by means of a match ; so he thought that on the way home he would stop at Mr. Level's house and ask Rainbow to give him .e matches. Rainbow often gave the boys ...atches to kindle their bonfires with, but always when he did so he charged them to be very careful of them, and never to light them near any buildings.

Rainbow gave Tommy two matches, with the usual injunction to be careful of them, and not to light them near the house. Tommy promised to be very careful indeed, and, taking the matches, he went away.

In walking across the yard he saw a small piece of paper lying on the ground.

" Ah !" said he to himself, " here is a piece of paper. I'll wrap my matches and my torpedoes in it, and then they will be very safe."

So he wrapped the torpedoes and the matches in the paper, and then, holding the parcel securely in his hand, he walked toward home.

It was now nearly night, and he was determined not to fire his torpedoes until the next morning. In fact, he did not know exactly how he was to go to work to fire them, though

he concluded that he was to light them in some
way by means of his matches. As it was now
nearly dark, he thought he could manage this
operation better in the morning, when it would
be light, and he could see to find the little *fuse*,
if there was one, attached to the torpedo. ꞏ
sides, he had some misgivings in respect to his
mother's being willing to have him play with
fire-works, unless he went away to some place
at a considerable distance from the house.
This he thought he could do better in the
morning.

Accordingly, when he reached his mother's
house, he went into the back yard, and walked
along through the yard toward the shed and
barn, holding his little parcel carefully in his
right hand. His intention was to find some
place to hide them until the next morning.

Just at this moment he heard a sound toward the street, and, looking round, he saw
Joseph, the man who worked for his mother,
coming along the road, mounted upon the back
of Lucky. Lucky had a bridle on, but no saddle. Joseph was riding him bareback. Joseph came into the yard, and rode up to the
place where Tommy was standing.

"Are you going to take Lucky to pasture,
Joseph?" asked Tommy.

L

"No," said Joseph, "it is too late. I'm going to let him stay in the barn to-night."

What Joseph called the barn was merely a small space partitioned off in the shed, where there was one stall, into which Lucky was often placed on such occasions as this. Above was a loft, where a small quantity of hay could be kept.

When Joseph arrived at the door leading into this little barn, he dismounted, and took the bridle off from Lucky's head. Lucky, as soon as he was free, walked into the barn, and proceeded at once to his stall. He expected to find something there to eat.

Tommy stood at the door of the stable looking in, and forgetting for the moment all about the pyrotechnics which he held in his hands. Joseph went up a ladder in the corner which led to the loft, in order to put down some hay for Lucky to eat.

As soon as he reached the top of the ladder, and turned to go into the loft, he disappeared from view, but in a moment Tommy heard his voice calling, "Tommy!"

"What!" said Tommy.

"Take up an armful of straw out of the corner, and spread it down in Lucky's stall, while I am giving him some hay."

Now Tommy liked very much to have something to do about the horse, and as Lucky was very gentle, and was never known to bite or to kick, it was safe for Tommy to go as near him as he pleased. Indeed, I think that Lucky took special care not to move his feet, or, at least, to move them very gently, whenever Tommy was near him, for fear of stepping upon him, or otherwise hurting him in some accidental manner.

Tommy went at once to the corner of the shed to take up an armful of straw. He had a sort of vague impression upon his mind that there was something in his hand which embarrassed him a little in taking up the straw, but he did not think of it distinctly. He stooped down and took up as much straw as he could grasp in his arms, keeping his right hand closed all the time upon the parcel containing the matches and the torpedoes.

"Stand round, Lucky!" said Tommy, in an authoritative voice, when he came to the stall, imitating the manner in which he had heard Joseph speak. "*Stand round!*"

Lucky stepped a little to one side with his hind feet, so that Tommy could get into the stall, and then went on eating the hay that Joseph was putting down into the manger for him.

Tommy began to sprinkle down the straw upon the floor of the stall, holding on all the time instinctively to his parcel, though by this time he had almost entirely forgotten that he had it in his hand. The operation would perhaps have gone on in this way quite successfully to the termination of it, had it not been that Lucky, forgetting perhaps that Tommy was there, suddenly stepped back nearer to the side where Tommy was standing, which led Tommy to drop every thing that he had in his hands, and place his hands open against the side of the horse in order to push him away.

"Stand over!" said Tommy, very authoritatively. "What are you about? Why don't you stand over?" The straw being now all upon the floor, Tommy came out of the stall, thinking that he had accomplished very successfully the work which Joseph had assigned him. He was not conscious of having dropped his fire-works — at least he was not distinctly conscious of it, though there was a vague feeling in his mind that he had left or forgotten something, he could not tell what, and it was not until Joseph came down from the loft, and was ready to go out of the barn, that he thought of his parcel, and, looking into his hand, he found that it was gone.

"I've dropped it somewhere," said Tommy to himself. "Where can it be?"

Tommy tried to remember when he last saw it or felt it in his hand. He could not remember having seen it since the time that Joseph came into the yard.

"I must have dropped it in the yard," said Tommy. "And I'll go and look, and if I can't find it there I'll go and look in the barn."

What Tommy ought to have done was to have told Joseph at once what had happened, and Joseph would have known what steps to take to recover the matches. But Tommy was afraid to do this. He had a sort of an idea that he had done wrong, and that he should get a scolding if he told any body that he had lost the matches.

It is very likely he would have got a scolding, for there are a great many persons who are indiscreet and unreasonable enough to scold children for mere accidents, or for occurrences of any kind which occasion them trouble, even when the children are not really to blame. So it is very probable that if he had told Joseph that he had had some matches and torpedoes in his hands a little while before, and that he had lost them somewhere, Joseph would have found fault with him for being so careless, or

would have told him that he had no business
to have any matches or torpedoes at all, and
particularly not to be carrying them in his hand
about the yard and barn.

At any rate, Tommy thought that he should
be able to find the parcel himself in the yard,
especially as the paper in which it was envel-
oped was white, and would accordingly show
very clearly among the grass, or upon the dark
surface of the ground.

" And if I can't find it in the yard," thought
Tommy to himself, " I'll come back and look`
for it in the barn.   It must be in the barn if it
is not in the yard."

Joseph came out of the barn and shut the
door.

" You'd better not fasten the door, Joseph,"
said Tommy.

" Why not ?" asked Joseph.

" Because perhaps Lucky may want to come
out," said Tommy.

"That's the very reason why I ought to fast-
en it," said Joseph.

" Why, if he wants to come out after he has
eaten his hay and lie down on the grass, or
walk about the yard, what harm will it do ?"
asked Tommy.

" I can't trust him," said Joseph.   " I have

not fastened him into his stall, and he can walk about the barn as much as he likes, but he must not come out into the yard."

So Joseph shut the door. There was a sort of hasp, with an oval opening in the end of it, which went over a staple, and there was a plug of wood fastened near by by a leather string, which was to be passed through the loop of the staple when the hasp was shut over it, and thus made the fastening secure. Such a wooden plug as this is called a fid.

Joseph put the hasp over the staple, and pinned it there with the fid, and then walked away, considering every thing secure. Tommy looked about the yard for some time, but the paper parcel was nowhere to be found. Then he went to the barn door. He tried to open it, but he could not. He looked up at the fastening, but it was beyond his reach.

"I *wish* that Joseph had not fastened the door," said he.

Tommy saw the end of the fid pointing down toward him through the loop of the staple.

"I'll get a stick," said he, "and push the fid up, and so let it drop out."

So he went and brought a stick, and by means of it he succeeded in pushing the fid up out of its place, so as to let it drop out upon one side, where it was held by the leather string to which it was suspended. Tommy then pushed the end of his stick behind the hasp and pried it out from the staple, and then he could easily open the door.

He went into the barn, but it had now begun to be pretty dark there, and it looked so lonesome that he did not dare to go in very far. He looked about upon the floor a little, but, not seeing his parcel any where, he concluded not to search for it any more that night, but to wait until the next morning.

So he went out of the barn and shut the door. He could not fasten it, however, for he could not reach; and, although the stick answered very well for pushing the fid out, it would by no means enable him to put it in again; so Tommy contented himself with shutting the door as closely as he could, and then went into the house, and shortly afterward he went to bed.

FIRE. 169

The door not secured. Opened by the wind.

CHAPTER XVI.

FIRE.

WHEN Tommy came out of the barn, after giving up the hope of finding the little parcel which he had dropped, he shut the door carefully, although he could not reach up to fasten it.

" Lucky never will know," he said to himself, " but that the fid is in. He will see that it is shut, and he never will think of trying to push it open."

It is not improbable that Lucky would have supposed that the door was fastened, and would have remained quietly in the barn all night, had it not been that about half past eleven o'clock, just as he had finished eating the hay which Joseph had given him, a gentle night breeze happened to spring up, and the wind, coming in through a small square window near the stall, pressed upon the outer door so as gently to force it open. The door moved slowly upon its hinges until it was about half open, and then stopped. A faint but very perceptible light shone in from the moon and stars. Lucky heard the movement from the door and saw the light, and he immediately conceived the idea that Joseph was coming to give him some more hay.

"He comes in just the right time," thought Lucky. "I have eaten all that he gave me, and I have not had quite enough."

So he turned his head round to see if Joseph were really coming; at the same time, he stepped to one side with his hind feet, so as to enable him to see better, and in so doing it happened that he stepped upon the paper parcel, which was lying upon the floor on one side of the stall among the straw. The iron of his shoe came with great weight upon the torpedoes, and it ground the sand into the fulminating powder with such force that both the torpedoes exploded, one an instant after the other.

Lucky was extremely terrified. He sprang out of the stall, and, as he turned round in doing so, it happened that his heels struck the parcel again, and this time they set one of the matches on fire. Lucky heard the hissing of the match, and this frightened him more than ever. He sprang across the barn, pushed out through the half-open door, galloped along the yard, bounded over the gate which Joseph had

FIRE. 171

Lucky's escape. He makes for Handie's yard. Why. Rainbow's plans.

taken the precaution to shut, and then, wheeling swiftly round, he went off toward Handie's
house at the top of his speed.

In the mean time the fire from the match
had caught into the straw, and was now gradually creeping along all over the floor of the
stall.

Lucky went on upon the full run until he
came to Handie's house, and then turned into
the yard and ran up to the back door, where
he suddenly stopped. The truth is, that Rainbow had been in the habit of feeding Lucky
on a little platform near the back door, in consequence of which Lucky liked very much to
go there. Indeed, the reason why Rainbow
adopted the plan of feeding him there was to
make him like to come, so that, if in any case
he should get away from Joseph or make his
escape into the road in any way, instead of
going off into the village or on the road, where
he would be likely to be taken up and put into
the pound, he would come at once into Handie's
yard, in hopes of finding something to eat on
Rainbow's platform.

The plan worked very well. Lucky liked
better to get into Handie's yard than to go to
any other place, and so, on this occasion, when
he found himself free in the road, after being

frightened out of the barn by the explosion of the torpedoes, he ran at once into the yard and galloped up to the back door. As soon as he got to the platform he put his fore feet up upon the edge of it, and began pawing there, as he was accustomed to do, in order to notify Rainbow that he was there, and to ask him to come out and give him something to eat.

Rainbow, who was sleeping quietly at this time in a little room over the shop, was awakened by the sound of horses' feet coming rapidly up the yard, and then by the pawing upon the platform.

"There's Lucky, I verily believe," said Rainbow, starting up in his bed. "What does he mean by coming here this time of night?"

Just then Rainbow saw a light gleaming in from a window on the back side of his room. He jumped out of bed and ran to the window, and saw a bright flame flashing out from the roof of Mrs. Blooman's barn, just over the place where Lucky's stall was situated.

Rainbow immediately ran to the door of Handie's room, and called out,

"Fire! Fire! Mr. Level, wake up! Mrs. Blooman's barn is on fire."

Rainbow slipped on his pantaloons and his shoes, and then went down stairs, three steps at a time, seized an axe which stood near the door, leaped over a fence, and ran across the orchard. In a few minutes he was followed by Handie, bringing a small ladder. By the time that they reached the house the family had been awakened. Joseph had come down, and was just ready to go to work. His first concern seemed to be on account of Lucky, whom he supposed to be in the barn; but Rainbow told him that Lucky was safe.

"He came galloping over into our yard," said Rainbow, hurriedly, "and waked me up to give the alarm."

Mrs. Blooman had come out too. She was half dressed, and holding Tommy in her arms, and so dreadfully frightened that she seemed not to know what to do or say.

"Don't be frightened," said Handie; "we can put the fire out. Put Tommy down on the grass, and go to the pump and pump water, and bring it out in the pail to Joseph. Don't pump too fast, and don't spill any of the water in bringing it."

Handie said this in so calm and quiet a tone that Mrs. Blooman was considerably reassured by his words. He then planted the ladder against the side of the house, and directed Joseph to carry up the water as fast as Mrs.

Blooman brought it out to him, and to throw it over the roof of the house on the side toward the fire.

"And now, Rainbow," said he, "come with me."

Handie immediately went to work, with Rainbow's assistance, to pull down the part of the shed which was between the barn and the house, so as to cut off and isolate the part which was on fire. They both mounted upon the roof, and began to rip off the boards, shingles and all, and to throw them down to the ground, as far as possible away from the fire. They took the boards off partly by means of the axe, and partly by means of an iron bar which Rainbow brought for that purpose.

"Work quietly," said Handie, whenever he found that Rainbow was getting too much excited. "We shall have time enough if we work quietly, but we shall not have half time enough if we get into a hurry and a worry."

By this time the alarm had spread, and several of the neighbors began to come. Of those who came thus to help, one, under Handie's direction, relieved Mrs. Blooman at the pump. Another stood at the foot, and another at the head of the ladder, to pass the buckets of water up to Joseph on the roof. Others took up the

INTERCEPTING THE FIRE.

FIRE. 177

Fire intercepted.   Its spreading prevented.   The danger soon over.

boards and pieces of joist from the ground as Handie and Rainbow threw them down, and carried them off to a place where they were beyond the reach of the fire. In this way, in a short time, the portion of the shed which intervened between the little barn and the house was entirely taken away, and the communication by which the house was chiefly endangered was cut off. The part that was on fire then quietly burned down. The men watched it, and they kept the flames in some degree subdued by throwing on water from time to time, and they took good care to keep the roof of the house, and the whole side that was toward the fire, constantly wet, so as to prevent its taking fire by any accidental spark.

Thus, in little more than an hour, the danger was entirely over. Mrs. Blooman and Tommy went back to bed, and Handie and Rainbow returned to their own house. As a matter of precaution, Joseph was left to watch the smouldering embers of the fire, to prevent their breaking out again, and he remained accordingly on the ground until the morning.

The next morning there was great inquiry made, and much interest manifested, to find out how the fire could have taken. Rainbow at once recollected the circumstance of his having

M

given Tommy some matches, and he suspected that those very matches had been, in some way or other, the cause of the fire. He determined to ask Tommy, and see if he could find out any thing from him about it.

Accordingly, when he came over to breakfast the next morning, he met Tommy in the yard looking at the remains of the fire, and, after some other conversation, he asked,

"Do you remember the matches I gave you last night, Tommy?"

"Yes," said Tommy, looking at the same time a little alarmed, "I remember them."

"Have you fired them off?" asked Rainbow.

"No," said Tommy, "I have not fired them off."

"What did you do with them?" asked Rainbow.

"I did not do any thing with them," said Tommy.

"Where are they, then? Give them to me," said Rainbow.

"I have not got them," added Tommy.

"Can't you go and get them?" asked Rainbow.

"Why—why—I have not found them yet," said Tommy. "But I'll go and find them now."

So saying, Tommy began to look about the yard to see if he could find his little parcel.

But he could not find it any where, and Rainbow, who went about with him trying to help him, continued to ask him questions while they were looking. He finally learned from Tommy that he came home the evening before with the matches and the torpedoes in his hand, all safely done up in the paper, and that he went into the barn to throw down some straw for Lucky, and that when he came out he could not find his matches any where, though he was sure he dropped them in the yard, for the last time that he remembered seeing them was when Joseph came into the yard on Lucky's back.

Rainbow had no doubt, from this statement, that Tommy had dropped his matches in the straw, and that they had taken fire there in some way, or that, perhaps, he had set them on fire himself in or near the barn, and that now he was afraid to tell the truth about it. At any rate, he had very little doubt that the matches which he had given to Tommy were, in some way or other, the cause of the fire.

He determined, however, that he would not say any thing about this.

"Poor little fellow!" said he to himself, "I don't believe that he was to blame; and he will

only get scoldings that he does not deserve if
the people think that he set the barn on fire.
It is true, he ought not to have gone near the
barn with his matches.   He promised me that
he would not, and so he was in fault in some
degree.   But it will not do any good for me to
tell of his fault, and so I will conceal it."

Accordingly, Rainbow said nothing, but went
to work clearing away the rubbish of the fire;
and when he heard others making inquiries
and conjectures in respect to the manner in
which the fire took, he went quietly on with
his work, and said not a word.

The motive which thus influenced Rainbow
to conceal Tommy's fault would seem at first
view a very good one, and it was, in fact, a good
one, though, as is usually the case with all our
good motives, there was mixed up with it something like a selfish consideration, after all.   He
had a secret feeling that he might perhaps be
blamed himself for having given Tommy the
matches, if it should be known or supposed
that the barn was set on fire in that way; so
that it was partly on his own account, and not
altogether from a charitable desire to conceal
the faults of others, that he concluded not to
reveal what he knew.

CHAPTER XVII.
THE CONCLUSION.

A DAY or two after these occurrences, Handie and Rainbow were speaking of the fire at Mrs. Blooman's, and Rainbow had been expressing his sorrow, on Mrs. Blooman's account, that she had met with such a loss, when Handie told him that she had not met with any loss at all.

"Not any loss at all?" said Rainbow, surprised. "How is that?"

"The house was insured," said Handie, "and the company that insured it are obliged to build up the part that was burned down, and make it as good as it was before, or else pay her the money that it will cost, and let her do it."

"And how about the part that we pulled down?" asked Rainbow.

"They are to pay for that too," said Handie. "The company's agent has been here to examine the case, and they estimate that it will cost them fifty dollars to make it all as good as it was before. So they have offered to repair the damage themselves, or to give Mrs. Blooman the fifty dollars and let her do it, whichever she pleases."

"And what is she going to do?" asked Rainbow.

"She is going to take the fifty dollars and get me to build up her shed and barn again. But she is going to put some money of her own to the fifty, and make a better barn than she had before."

"That will be an excellent plan," said Rainbow.

"So, you see," continued Handie, "she does not lose any thing by the fire; unless, indeed," he added, "she loses Joseph in consequence of it."

"How can she lose Joseph?" asked Rainbow.

"Why, she thinks," continued Handie, "that Joseph must have set the barn on fire—not on purpose, but by some sort of carelessness. He was the last person that was there that night, and Mrs. Blooman thinks he went in smoking his pipe, or doing something of that sort. He says that he did not take his pipe in, or any thing else that could possibly have set the hay on fire, but Mrs. Blooman does not believe him. In fact, there is one thing that he says that she knows is not true."

" What is that?" asked Rainbow.

" Why, he says," replied Handie, "that he shut the door when he came out, and fastened it securely by putting the fid into the hasp. Now this can't be true; for, if the door had been fastened, how could Lucky have got out ?"

" Perhaps somebody might have unfastened it afterward," suggested Rainbow.

" There was nobody there to do it," said Handie—" nobody except Tommy, and he could not reach."

Here there was a pause. Rainbow seemed to be reflecting upon what he had heard.

" And what is Mrs. Blooman going to do ?" he said, at length.

" She is going to send Joseph away. She says she does not wish to keep any body about her premises that she finds does not tell the truth."

This conversation with Handie changed the whole state of the case in Rainbow's mind in respect to the propriety of his concealing what he knew about Tommy and the matches. He saw now that if it was really true that Tommy had been the means of setting the barn on fire, the concealment of that fact would be no longer an act of charity. It would be an act of injustice. It would be the means of bringing an unmerited stain upon Joseph's character, as well as of depriving him of his place. He determined immediately to talk with Tommy on the subject again, to see if he could not find out certainly what he did with his matches. He, however, determined not to make the inquiry directly, for fear of alarming Tommy, and thus preventing him from speaking freely.

That day, when he went to dinner, he met Tommy in the yard. Tommy had a little kite, and he was trying to disentangle the tail of it.

"Come here to the steps of the door, Tommy," said Rainbow, "and I'll help you untangle your kite-tail."

So Tommy followed Rainbow to the door, and both of them sat down on the steps.

"Did it frighten you to see the barn on fire the other night?" asked Rainbow.

"Yes," said Tommy, "it frightened me very much indeed."

"Do you think it frightened Lucky?" asked Rainbow.

"Yes," said Tommy; "and if it had not been for me, he would have been burned all up."

"How so?" asked Rainbow.

"Because, if it had not been for me, he could not have got out," said Tommy.

"Did you let him out?" asked Rainbow.

"I unfastened the door," said Tommy. "I told Joseph not to fasten him in, but he would, and afterward I unfastened him."

"How did you do it?" asked Rainbow. "I should not think you could reach."

"I could not reach with my hands," said Tommy, "and so I took a stick. I took a stick and pushed the fid out."

"What did you unfasten the door for?" asked Rainbow.

"Because I wanted to go in," said Tommy.

"What did you want to go in for?" asked Rainbow, speaking all the time in an indifferent and unconcerned tone, and going on with his work of disentangling the kite-tail.

"Why, I wanted to go in the barn," said Tommy.

"What did you want to go in *for?*" asked Rainbow.

"Why—why—I wanted," said Tommy, hesitating, and then speaking in a low and timid tone of voice, "I wanted to see if I could not find my torpedoes."

"Your torpedoes?" asked Rainbow.

"Yes," said Tommy, "and my matches. I wrapped them up together in a paper, and I ·
had them in my hand, and Joseph told me to put some straw down in Lucky's stall, and I

did, and then I could not find my parcel any
where."

"Perhaps you dropped it among the straw."

"No," said Tommy.

"Are you sure?" asked Rainbow.

"Yes," said Tommy, "I am perfectly sure."

"Then where do you think you did drop
it?" asked Rainbow.

"I don't know," said Tommy, shaking his
head doubtfully.

Rainbow was now well convinced that Tommy had dropped his matches in the barn, and
that the fire had been set in that way. So he
at once determined that, in justice to Joseph, he
would explain to Handie all that he knew
about the affair.

"I suppose," said he, "that I shall be blamed
for giving Tommy the matches, and that he
will get a scolding for carrying them into the
barn ; but this will be better than to have Joseph lose his character and his place when he
is entirely innocent."

Rainbow accordingly lost no time in explain-
ing the case to Handie, and Handie explained
it to Mrs. Blooman. He had no doubt, he said,
that Tommy dropped his matches somewhere
in the barn, and that afterward Lucky set them
on fire by treading upon them when he was

walking about. Mrs. Blooman was satisfied herself that that was the true explanation of the origin of the fire, and all her suspicions of Joseph were consequently removed.

Rainbow was mistaken, however, in suppos-ing that he and Tommy would suffer in con-sequence of its being made known that the fire was occasioned by their joint imprudence. Handie thought that the affair would of itself make Rainbow more careful in future, without his saying any thing for the purpose of special-ly enforcing the lesson, so he said nothing at all. As for Mrs. Blooman, she was, on the whole, glad of the fire, on account of its en-abling her to build up her barn and shed bet-ter than they were before, without losing the value of the old building. Accordingly, al-though she acquitted Joseph entirely of having had any thing to do with the origin of the fire, she said she did not know whether Tommy was the rogue or not, and she did not much care.

Handie continued for some weeks at The Three Pines, until he had put the buildings in perfect order. He made the place so attractive that it was engaged by a good tenant before he quite got through with his work. After he

had completed the repairs of his own house, he
went to work to make a new barn for Lucky
in the rear of Mrs. Blooman's house, and to re-
build the shed.   Lucky was extremely pleased
with his new quarters when they were finished
and he was taken in for the first time to see his
new stall.

In respect to Lucky's history, however, sub-
sequent to this time, a more full account will
be given in the next volume of this series of
stories, which will be entitled SELLING LUCKY.

In due time Handie and Rainbow went home
to their own native town.   There was only one
thing that marred Rainbow's satisfaction in returning to his mother, and that was his disap-
pointment in not being able to take Pineapple
with him, as he fully intended to do during all
the time that he resided at The Three Pines.
Pineapple was a very docile and intelligent cat,
and Rainbow became very much attached to
her, and it was on this account that he intended to take her home with him when he returned to his mother's.   But, with all the excellen-
cies of her character, Pineapple had one very
serious fault, which was the means at last of
bringing her to an untimely end.

This fault was the habit of going about late
at nights among the neighbors, to walk over

the wood-piles and roofs there, and to
quaintances with other cats that she was
tomed to encounter in these nocturnal ram
The reason why she liked to be out thus .
night was because all boys and all dogs were
asleep at that time, and she could go where she
pleased without meeting with any body to mo-
lest her.

Now it happened that at one of the neighbors' houses there was a shed with a wood-pile
in it, and the girl who lived there, in taking the
wood from the pile, would take it from the
lower part, where she could easily reach it, thus
leaving what was above in a very steep pile,
until at length it fell of itself, when the portion
below which supported it had been sufficiently
taken away. Of course, when it was ready to
fall, she would pull out the stick below, and
then step back out of the way, and so escape
the danger of its falling upon her head. Sometimes, however, she would take away so much
of the wood below that the part above was just
ready to fall, and then would go away, leaving
it in that condition.

She did this without reflecting on the danger
that some child might pass by, and be very se-
riously hurt by the pile falling down upon
him.

...appened that one night, a short ...ore Rainbow was going home, Pineap- ...vas walking about this very shed, near ...night, at a time when the pile had been left . the state above described. Pineapple attempted to walk up; for, however steep the face ... pile might be, it was very easy for ... up by taking hold of the sides and ... ...e wood with her claws. She ascend- ... thus without any difficulty until she almost reached the top, when at length her weight proved too much for the projecting mass of wood above, which was before just ready to fall. The whole pile came down with a prolonged and rattling crash, which would have been heard in the house if the people had not been very sound asleep. Poor Pineapple was instantly killed by the mass of heavy sticks which fell upon her, and she was buried so deep under the wood that even her body was not found until four or five days after Rainbow had gone.

THE END.